A Second Chance, College Football Romance

Kaci Rose

Five Little Roses Publishing

Contents

Copyright	I
Blurb	II
	IV
Get Free Books!	V
1. Prologue	1
2. Chapter 1	8
3. Chapter 2	18
4. Chapter 3	35
5. Chapter 4	47
6. Chapter 5	57
7. Chapter 6	68
8. Chapter 7	81

9. Chapter 8	87
10. Chapter 9	101
11. Chapter 10	112
12. Chapter 11	120
13. Chapter 12	129
14. Chapter 13	136
15. Chapter 14	145
16. Chapter 15	162
17. Chapter 16	174
18. Chapter 17	183
19. Chapter 18	198
20. Chapter 19	208
21. Chapter 20	219
22. Chapter 21	228
23. Chapter 22	241
24. Chapter 23	254

25. Chapter 24	263
26. Chapter 25	275
27. Chapter 26	282
28. Chapter 27	295
29. Chapter 28	304
30. Chapter 29	311
31. Epilogue	326
See all of Kaci Rose's Books	339
Connect with Kaci Rose	341
Please Leave a Review!	342

Copyright © 2020, by Kaci Rose. All Rights Reserved.

No part of this publication may be reproduced, distributed, or transmitted in any form or by any means, including photocopying, recording, or other electronic or mechanical methods, or by any information storage and retrieval system without the prior written permission of the publisher, except in the case of very brief quotations embodied in critical reviews and certain other noncommercial uses permitted by copyright law.

Publisher's Note: This is a work of fiction. Names, characters, places, and incidents are a product of the author's imagination. Locales and public names are sometimes used for atmospheric purposes. Any resemblance to actual people, living or dead, or to businesses, companies, events, institutions, or locales is completely coincidental.

Book Cover By: **Sarah Kil Creative Studio**

Editing By: Nikki @ **Indie Hub**

Blurb

A football player, a secret crush, and the Hail Mary text that would change everything...

Avery had no idea who the mystery text came from, but she owed them a thank you. Because of their message, she showed up at a party for the football team and caught her boyfriend cheating. But the messages didn't stop there. Whoever the person she nicknamed 'Titan' truly was, they offered her support and friendship when she needed it most. Now, she finds herself longing to meet her hero face-to-face.

Denver isn't sure if Avery even remembers the kiss they shared freshman year, but he's thought about it every day since. As much as he wanted to be with her, family obligations pulled him away. It was torture watching her date another member of his football team, yet he never would have intervened if they were happy. One thing he wouldn't do was stand back and watch as his buddy cheated on her time and again. When it's revealed that he is her mysterious 'Titan', Denver prays it will be the beginning of his second chance.

But his family responsibilities haven't lessened. And her trust in football players has been destroyed. Can the pair score a touchdown into their happily-ever-after under the scrutiny of the stadium lights?

This is a Steamy, Small Town, College Football Romance. No Cliffhangers.

As always, there is a satisfying happy ever after.

If you love steamy romances with insta love, hot love scenes, small towns, and football, then this one is for you.

To all those waiting for their second chance.

Get Free Books!

Do you like Cowboys? Military Men? Best friends brothers? What about sweet, sexy, and addicting books?

If you join Kaci Rose's Newsletter you get these books free!

Join Kaci Rose's newsletter and get your free books!

Now on to the story!

Prologue

Avery

College is the time to do stupid things and make mistakes. That's what Mom told me when she dropped me off last week. Although, I'm not sure she meant the kind of mistake I made tonight at the welcome freshman party.

My roommate Kelsey and I bonded almost instantly over our love for Outlander, both the TV show and the books. We also love watching The Big Bang Theory when nothing else is on.

So, it made sense when she suggested attending this party that we go together. It's part of the college experience and we made a vow on day one to have as many college experiences as possible.

The party is more of a bonfire gathering, but the whole football team is here. The music is good, and the food isn't bad. Mountain Gap University is known for its food. It might be their Southeast Tennessee roots.

I am at the food table picking up another fried chicken slider when the handsomest guy I've ever seen comes over. He walks over with a confidence that seems to dwindle once he's in front of me. He shoves his hands into the pockets of his jeans and looks at his feet. His dark blue Mountain Gap Football shirt stretches across his chest, showing he has the kind of muscular football players body all the girls drool after. "Those any good?" he asks, holding my gaze with the most gorgeous green eyes.

I grin and look down at the food in my hand. "This is my fourth one. I can't seem to stop myself, so yeah."

He smiles. "I'm Denver." He's quite a bit taller than me and when I look up something draws me to him, making me want to know more.

"Hi, I'm Avery."

"Nice to meet you, Avery. Where you from?"

"Nashville."

"You didn't want to go to school there?" He grabs a few of the sliders.

"My mom and dad came here and met each other, so did my dad's parents. I figured I'd carry on the tradition. What about you?"

"Cookeville, it's an hour north of here."

"Football player? I'm assuming." I point to his shirt.

He laughs. "Yeah been playing since I was about ten."

"Your dream to play football here?"

"Well, the coach here was a Tennessee Titans player, and a good one. I wanted to learn from him. I had my pick of schools with my football scholarship, but I wanted to play for the best."

"And Mountain Gap Football is the best."

"They've won more national championships than any other college."

"Impressive."

"So, I'm going to be honest and hope you'll help me out. The football team has a tradition of having freshmen do dares at the freshman party. My dare was to come over here and kiss you. My momma raised a gentleman so I'm asking for your help."

"You're asking my permission to kiss me?"

He laughs and rubs the back of his neck, looking at the ground before looking back up at me. "Yeah, I guess I am."

"College experiences," I whisper and shake my head.

"What?"

"Nothing. I guess I can help you out. A simple kiss, nothing more."

"Promise." His eyes lock with mine. His hand moves to my waist as he gently pulls me closer and his lips land on mine.

I'm expecting a sweet simple kiss, but from the second his lips touch mine it's like he's lit a live wire. Flames travel across my skin. He moans into my mouth and brings his free hand up to cup the back of my head and deepen the kiss. I gasp from the sensation and place my hand on his chest to steady myself.

I've never been kissed like this before. I hold on to him for dear life. This is the kiss all the romance books talk about, one that my mom describes when she kissed my dad for the first time. When the kiss softens, I can't seem to catch my breath.

"Avery," he whispers against my lips. The moment is shattered by a cell phone ringing and Denver pulls back to take his phone from his pocket.

"I have to take this." He looks at me like he doesn't want to leave, like he is waiting for me to say something, but I have no idea what. "Wait here for me?"

I nod and he walks off, talking to whoever just interrupted the best kiss of my life.

I touch my lips thinking about that kiss, his lips; the heat between us was unlike anything I've ever felt in my life. But it was all for a dare. Wait until my mom hears this one, it should make her happy until at least Halloween when I know she will demand I dress up and attended at least one Halloween party.

"Hey, are you okay?" a male voice asks, breaking me from my daydream. I turn and find another guy in the team football shirt behind me.

"Oh, yeah I'm fine."

"That was kind of a dick move."

"I don't know what you mean."

"He kissed you like that and then walked off. Probably to take a call from his girlfriend he was talking about earlier."

My stomach sinks; of course, the gorgeous football player has a girlfriend. He was honest with me though; it was a kiss for a dare. No matter how it felt. Apparently, he didn't feel the same.

"It was a dare, wasn't it? I know how the football team works." He smiles and looks at his feet. "Yeah, that was a shitty thing to do. I'm Kyle, also a freshman but I swear I'm not here on any dare."

"I'm Avery. What was your dare?"

"To get a cheerleader's phone number. I got it and gave it to a senior on the team. I'm not interested."

"Isn't every football player interested in the cheerleaders?"

He grins. "No. We don't all fit the stereotype."

Kyle is easy to get along with, and we talk a good part of the night and part ways with plans for dinner next week.

Chapter 1

Denver

I'm in my room trying to study when the sounds of someone stumbling up the stairs pull me from my book.

"Kyle!" I hear someone squeal, and a high-pitched giggle fills the room. Great, Kyle brought home another girl *and* he's still dating Avery. They have been dating since they were freshmen, but over the summer he started sleeping around, saying that junior year is the year to have fun. I suggested he break up with Avery, but he laughed and said there was no need since the team will keep his secrets.

I know the coach would have my ass if I outed him. He is always going on and on about trust and how the team falls apart without it.

I still think of that kiss with Avery in freshman year. I have never felt anything like it. Then my mom called and needed help. She's single and it's always been just me and her. She worked hard so I could play football, but in my senior year of high school I started to make a name for myself. The good is always followed by the bad it seems. My popularity drew attention to Mom, and she seems to have developed a stalker. We've gone to the police and they say they can't do anything because he's just left notes and gifts on her doorstep with no real threats but enough veiled ones to scare her.

When I bailed the night of the freshman party, I drove the hour home and helped her move to a new place outside town that was a bit safer. With the help of my mom's best friend I put the lease in my name so it can't be tracked as easily, and made my mom take some self-defense classes.

I wish I could get her into a high-security building, but money is tight with me in school. I can't work since I'm here on a football scholarship, but I have a room at the football house and food is taken care of. My mom still works to pay for things like my cell phone bill and any extras I need.

I've been going home when I can, taking jobs around the neighborhood, mowing lawns for cash to help Mom out. I add the money to her wallet, and she pretends she doesn't know I do it.

After I helped Mom get settled after the incident that night, I went straight back to Avery, but by then she had gone off with Kyle. It hurt to watch them together and see her smile at him. They seemed happy and as long as she was happy, I stayed away, but no other girl has held any appeal for me. I haven't dated, kissed, or even slept with anyone since that night I kissed Avery. Even though we're not together, it just feels wrong to be with someone else.

It doesn't matter what I say though, the Jersey Chasers still surround me wherever I go. Now Kyle is taking advantage of those opportunities, it's harder to stay away from Avery. I've tried to talk to her, but she doesn't want anything to do with me. Part of me wonders if she remembers that kiss.

I'm trying to concentrate on reading this book for class, but my mind keeps returning to Avery. She is every part the southern belle from Tennessee you would expect. Angelic blonde hair in waves down her back, rich milk-chocolate eyes, and a smile that lights up her whole face.

I toss my book down on my desk, it's useless trying to study any more tonight. I head out to the loft on the third-floor landing where my room is, to get some water, and notice Kyle has left his keys and his phone on the coffee table.

His phone that has Avery's number programmed into it.

I shouldn't touch it, I know that. Thinking I'll be stopped by a password on his phone, I'm shocked when there isn't one. What an idiot. I find Avery's number and see several unanswered messages from her tonight. I add her number to my phone and head back to my room.

Before I can talk myself out of it, I take a chance, a hail Mary pass.

Me: Avery?
Avery: Who is this?
Me: A friend.

She sends a laughing emoji.

Avery: How did you get my number?
Me: From your boyfriend.
Avery: He gave it to you?
Me: No. I might have taken it without him knowing. He needs to put a password on his phone.

There are a few minutes where I start to doubt myself before she replies.

Avery: So, are you a football player?
Me: Yes.
Avery: Have I met you before?

Good lord, have we met? I want to tell her we met when she turned my world upside down and I made the dumbest move ever by walking away from her. But I can't find the right words.

Me: Yes.

Great, one-word answers, it's a miracle she's still talking to me.

Avery: Okay, tell me something about you.

I know at this moment that I need to tell her the truth, because I know I can't tell her who I am. So, when this all blows up in my face, I can at least say I never once lied to her in our texts.

I don't see this ending any other way. If Kyle finds out I don't even want to think of it will affect the team.

Me: I'm tired of the football player stereotype. So many guys use it to their advantage, even when in relationships.

Like your boyfriend Kyle, I want to add, but I know I can't. I wait for the three bubbles to pop up to tell me she's typing and when they don't, I send another text with the hope to keep her talking.

Me: Hence why I am holed up in my room alone again while they are all out doing their thing.

Finally, the three bubbles pop up.

Avery: Spend a lot of time alone?
Me: Every night.
Avery: So, you know me already. I feel like it's only fair I get to know you because, like you, I am holed up in my room alone tonight. So bored!
Me: No Boyfriend?
Avery: No, he has a light training session with a few teammates. You aren't with them?
Me: No, I did some training earlier today because I had a paper to finish.

Some training session. I'm sure his endurance is improving, and I don't doubt he was out with some team makes when he met Giggles. A great way at twisting words, Kyle. How many other lies has he told her that she doesn't know about?

Me: Well, if we are going to get to know each other, let's make a promise: Never lie to each other. Always be honest and open.

Avery: Deal. So, you're a football player. Is your plan to play for the NFL?

Me: Yeah, I guess so. I know a year in the NFL would provide the financial security I want and that my mom needs.

Avery: If money wasn't an issue, what would you do?

Me: I'm good at football so I'd love to coach. That's what I'm hoping to do after my NFL time. Now the same question to you. What do you plan to do and what would you do if money wasn't a factor?

Avery: I'd love to write books all day. Get lost in new worlds. Instead, I'm going to be a copywriter and sell people things they don't need or never knew they needed. If you could pick any NFL team to get drafted to, which one would you pick?

Me: Tennessee Titans.

Avery: Why?

Me: It's not here, it's not back home, but it's still in the south, still in Tennessee. I've been to Nashville a few times and I think my mom would really like it there.

Avery: Seems fitting. As I don't know your name, I think I'll call you Titan.
Me: I like that. Well, it's late, you need to get to sleep, beautiful.

Shoot. She isn't mine and calling her beautiful is crossing yet another line, but it just slipped out and felt right.

Avery: Okay, and you need sleep for practice.

Yeah, I won't be getting any sleep tonight. I already know I'm going to read these messages over and over until I have every word memorized. I'll picture her lying in bed texting me.

Me: Don't worry about me. I will always have time for you.
Avery: You're a football player. Don't make promises you can't keep.

Dammit, Kyle. How much has he fucked up any chance I might ever have with her based on the simple fact that I'm a football player?

Me: I don't make promises I can't keep. You will learn that about me. I PROMISE I will always have time for you.

Avery: Okay, goodnight, Titan.

Me: Goodnight, Avery.

Chapter 2

Avery

I wake up to the smell of bacon and coffee. I know Kelsey is cooking because she wants to hear the story, I have to tell her. She was out late last night on a date, so I texted her after I said good night to Titan and said I have a juicy guy story for her. I fell asleep before she got home. I know she'll be trying to bribe me with breakfast. It's totally working. I'm such a sucker for bacon.

I get up and make my way to the kitchen. Kelsey and I share a two-bedroom apartment across the street from campus. It's a highly sought after building but my parents nailed it down for me. They were so proud of me for getting a full scholarship and said they had the money for college saved up and wanted me to use it for a good apartment.

Mom insisted I do freshman year in the dorms, for the experience. I'm glad she did because it's how I met Kelsey. I had planned to stay by myself in a nice quiet one-bedroom, but Kelsey and I bonded in the dorms, so when my parents mentioned a two-bedroom was open, I told them to grab it and I invited Kelsey to move in with me.

She insisted on paying rent, so I've been putting the money into a savings account for her. It will be her graduation gift. I don't need the money. My grandmother passed away last year and left me everything, including her house in Nashville, which needs some work.

My dad grew up in that house but said he and mom saved up money to buy their house and it holds so much meaning to them they couldn't leave it. Plus, Grandma's place is huge, and my parents are traveling a lot now, so they don't need the space. They say I do because apparently, I will be giving them ten grandbabies. Yes, my mom has said the number ten specifically.

"Hey, girl! You were fast asleep last night when I got home. Grab some coffee, pancakes, and bacon for your juicy guy story!"

"Deal." I barely sit down at the table before she sets the food down in front of me.

"Okay, spill!" She nearly bounces out of her seat as I get my first strip of bacon down.

"So last night, I was about to go to sleep when my phone goes off." I hand her my phone and let her read the texts from Titan. This is easier than explaining, and it buys me some time to eat before she starts asking a million questions.

"Do you have any idea who it is?"

"No, there are what, ninety guys on the football team? I've met most if not all of them in passing at some point."

"One hundred and eleven."

"What?"

"There are one hundred and eleven guys on the football team."

"I don't want to know how you know that."

"So, it's a guy who likes you, but because of the football brother code won't make a move so he's reached out anonymously. Oh my gosh, Av, it's so romantic!"

I roll my eyes. Kelsey is a hopeless romantic. She thinks true love will be like it is on the Hallmark Channel, all sweet and perfect in a huge glitter bow.

"What should I do? I have a boyfriend."

"Who treats you like crap."

"Kelsey..."

"Okay, okay." She throws her hands up in surrender. She is very vocal about not liking Kyle and thinking I can do better than him, and how if he cared he would make time for me. I know he's concentrating on football; the NFL is his dream and he has to give it his all.

"But think about this, while Kyle was *so* busy with 'training'" She makes air quotes. "Titan here made time to text you."

I won't admit that thought did cross my mind. My phone pings before my mind can go down that road again.

Titan: Good morning, beautiful. Have a good day today.

A good morning text? When was the last time Kyle sent me a good morning text? Well over a year. No, dammit. Avery, don't go down that road.

Me: Thanks. Morning class today, then work.

Titan: I have class then training and prep for this weekend's game.

"Is that Titan?"

"Yeah."

"Look at that huge smile on your face."

I didn't even know I was smiling. I drop the smile when I look up at her.

"Girl, it's okay, have some fun with Titan, but think about how he can text you good morning. Where is Kyle? You know my feelings on him, so I'll drop it, but I haven't seen you smile like that in a while."

Me: Away game, right?

Titan: Yes. Thankfully, a short travel day.

Me: What position do you play?

Titan: Nice try.

Me: Can't blame a girl for trying.

Titan: Have a good day, Avery.

Me: You too.

I get up and get ready for class, pour a to-go cup of coffee, and head out. I love being able to walk to class from my apartment. It allows me to take in the fresh air and the world around me. Well, I like it until it snows, anyway.

I pull out my phone to see if I have anything from Titan. Or Kyle because really, I should be wishing for a text from my boyfriend, not some mystery football player. I'm not paying attention when I run into a hard, warm wall.

"Whoa, careful there."

I'd know that voice anywhere. Denver Bolter. The guy who kissed me freshman year and then disappeared. He's been nothing but nice to me since, and he was upfront that the kiss was just for a bet, so I can't be mad at him. I mean, I was pretty mad at first, but three years later I'm over it.

He is the most popular football player and as Kelsey likes to tell me, the hottest by far. She still can't believe I kissed him freshman year. He is always surrounded by Jersey Chasers and Kelsey is convinced he's a player and sleeps around. I try not to pay attention to the rumors.

"Sorry, I have a lot on my mind today, I wasn't paying attention." I take a step back.

"Well, we're heading the same way, I feel like I should walk you to make sure you get there safe."

Before I can agree, Kyle walks up and acts like he didn't forget to call me last night like he said he would.

"Hey, babe. That coffee for me?" He grabs the coffee from my hand and starts drinking. In a split second, I catch Denver's jaw clench before his face relaxes.

"What the fuck, Kyle?" I grit out.

"Well, it was a long night, ugh, what with training and all, baby. Now hug me so you can get to class." He winks at Denver before reaching for me.

When the hell did Kyle get so cocky and condescending?

I go in to give him a hug, but the hickey on his neck catches my eye. I tense up but he hugs me anyway not even noticing how stiff I am. Soon as he lets me go, I bolt for class without saying goodbye to either of them.

Things haven't been adding up for weeks. Kyle is always busy, but like Kelsey pointed out, Titan had the time to talk to me. Kyle's spot on the team isn't the best and he doesn't have as hard of a training schedule as some of the other guys, like Denver who is one of the best running backs in the NCAA right now.

I've had this feeling in my gut for weeks, but why doesn't the hickey shock me so much? Why do I have so little emotion over it? I try to push it aside as I walk into class and take my seat in the middle row.

A few minutes later Denver walks in, his eyes lock on mine. Did he see the hickey too? Does he know that Kyle was lying about his training last night? Denver's eyes have me under a spell, but it's broken when Jersey Chasers surround him before he even sits down.

I watch him and he looks uncomfortable. One girl places a hand on his shoulder, and he reaches up to remove it. He tries to ignore them and doesn't flirt. This doesn't strike me as the moves of the player that Kelsey keeps saying he is.

I pull out my phone and send off a quick text to Kelsey about what just happened with Kyle before I forget to tell her.

Kelsey: Did you confront him?
Me: No, I was almost late for class.
Kelsey: When will you say something?
Me: I don't know, I don't have the energy for that right now. Can we talk tonight?
Kelsey: I'll have wine.

I tuck my phone away as the professor walks in.

***

I've just finished with the 4 p.m. rush at the coffee shop on campus where I work part-time. I like my job and after grandma passed, I wanted my normal routine, so I just kept working. The last customer just walks out when my phone vibrates letting me know I have a text message.

Titan: You work at the coffee shop, right?

Me: Yes, stalker...

Titan: What is your favorite drink there?

Me: Most days just a plain coffee but I do like the frozen mocha on a hot day. What kind of coffee do you drink?

Titan: Plain coffee but I do like a peppermint hot chocolate around Christmas time. Do I lose man points for that?

Me: Nope, I love getting a peppermint hot chocolate and driving around to look at Christmas lights in the winter.

Titan: That sounds like a tradition I should be starting.

Me: Maybe by Christmas, you'll tell me who you are, and we can go together.

Titan: Maybe. Okay, training time. Later, coffee girl.

***

We spend the next week texting almost nightly. He sends me random questions asking my favorite food, colors, sports team, TV shows, and movies. Random questions like steak or seafood, sweet tea or unsweet, and even silly ones like which way is the correct way to put the toilet paper roll on.

He sends me funny Big Bang Theory memes and videos, and we talk about our childhood and what high school was like.

Saturday night I get one of my nightly texts, but it shakes me.

Titan: Hey, are you here?
Me: Where?
Titan: The football party. I saw Kyle so I assumed you'd be here.

Me: Didn't even know there was a football party.

Kelsey comes barging in just then. "Hey, are we going to the football party tonight?"

"Well, I didn't know there was a football party until just now, so I'd say no."

I watch her face fall and I know she is thinking the same thing I am. Why didn't Kyle invite me, or even tell me about it?

We sit down to watch TV and there's radio silence for an hour. I can't shake the feeling I have. It's a nagging at the back of my head that there was more behind Titan's text. Why wouldn't my boyfriend invite me to a huge football party? Unless whoever is behind the hickey is there.

Me: Is there something I need to see?

He doesn't answer and I know he's trying to stick to the football code.

Me: You said no lies, always honest and open. Or does that only apply outside of football like every other guy?

Titan: No lies. Yes, you should be here.

"Get dressed, we are going to the party," I announce and jump up.

"YES!" Kelsey squeals and runs to her room. I know she already knows what she will wear. It won't take her long.

One thing I love about Kelsey is she is just as low maintenance as I am, so thirty minutes later we are out the door. We choose to walk because the football house is only a few blocks away.

"You know I've never liked Kyle. He treated you well at first, but last year something changed. Just a gut feeling that's made me not trust him. I think it started when he didn't go with you to your grandma's funeral. I don't like that he never has time for you, then this last week I see how much Titan can find time to text you, but your own boyfriend can't. That doesn't sit well with me, Av."

"I know, and it's been on my mind ever since I saw that hickey on Kyle's neck last week. I haven't seen him or talked to him more than a few texts and one phone call.

Do you think he is at the party with another girl in front of everyone?"

Kyle has been into some questionable things lately. Steroids for one. He says they perfectly legal, but I did some digging on school policy and the NCAA rules. and they aren't. He doesn't know that I know. I've kept my mouth shut even from Kelsey about them.

"Yes. I'm sorry, but I do. How do you feel about that?"

"Honestly, I want to just end it, even if he isn't with someone else. It's just been easier to ignore it because it's too much effort to deal with breaking up with him, but it's time. I know it. Plus, I always felt it should be done face to face."

"Good for you. I'm not leaving your side tonight."

"Thanks, girl."

"I got your back!"

We walk around the corner and the bright lights of the football house fill the street, the sounds of the music and noise from the crowd fill the air.

Me: We are walking up now.
Titan: Back porch.
Me: Thanks.

The closer we get to the football house, the louder the party gets. I know I'm going to have a killer headache tomorrow from all the loud music. Kelsey and I went to many parties our freshman year for the '*experience*', but it quickly became one of our least favorite experiences. Since freshman year we only go to one or two a year. We walk through the front door and my senses are assaulted with flashing lights, loud music, and cheap beer.

Denver is by the door with a sad look on his face. He nods at me when I walk in. I smile as Kelsey takes my hand, so we don't get separated as we make our way through several crowded rooms to the back porch.

A few of the players seemed shocked to see me but mask their faces quickly, thinking I didn't see their expressions. I'm not drunk, so I saw them just fine. This all confirms what I'm about to walk into. My nerves start to take over, mostly because I know a confrontation is coming.

As we step out on to the back porch, the cool night air covers my skin and it's a welcome relief from the hot stuffy air inside. I look around the back porch until I spot Kyle on the porch swing with not one, but two girls, one of them with her hand down his pants and the other one's hands all over him from behind.

"Wow," I breathe out, and walk over to them, stopping right in front of the swing.

Kyle jumps up, dumping the girls on the ground and adjusting his clothing.

"I think I'm more shocked about you getting two girls at once, than you actually cheating on me." I can't help but laugh at the situation.

"It's not what you think, baby."

"Or it's exactly what I think. I've known for weeks. I've seen the hickeys, I've just been too tired from dealing with school, work, and my grandma's estate to dump your ass like I should have. But we are *long* over."

"How did you even find out about the party?" he asks, anger hardening his voice. It looks like he is done trying to suck up. That didn't last long.

"It's a *football* party the whole campus knows about it. It's a *huge* red flag when you don't invite your girlfriend, asshole."

"Whatever, like a football player would actually be interested in you," he sneers. Well, I can play dirty too.

"You think you'd actually be getting laid if you weren't a football player? Your dick is nothing to write home about, and you have no clue how to use it. But these girls are just looking to attach themselves to a name for the money. They won't care about your lack of skill in that department. Have fun."

With that, I turn to storm out.

Chapter 3

Denver

When I saw Kyle here tonight, I thought I'd get to see Avery, even if it was from across the room. When I realized she didn't even know about the party, I knew the question was coming. I promised her honesty, but I'd also promised to be loyal to my team. Avery is a good girl though, and she doesn't deserve this. I know my momma would kick my ass if she knew I didn't take Avery's side, and my momma means more to me than football. Avery means more to me than football.

When she showed up, she looked so beautiful, it hurt me knowing what she was going to walk in on. I followed her to the back, I wanted to see how it went down and be there if she needed me. I didn't expect how well that girl can hold her own.

As she turns to walk away, Kyle lunges and grabs her wrist, yanking her back.

"Let go," she yells, trying to pull her wrist away.

"Kyle, man, let her go. If coach finds out you grabbed her like that, he will bench you." I step up closer to them, no longer watching from the sidelines.

"Why? You going to tell him?" he challenges.

"No." I look around. "But not everyone on this porch is loyal to you." Avery has drawn quite a crowd and I'm sure coach will hear about this in detail by Monday.

He lets her go. "You're not worth it."

"Neither were you!" she snaps and grabs her friend's hand, heading back into the house.

I give Kyle a quick look, shaking my head at the stupid situation he's got himself into, then head in after them. I set my untouched beer down and catch up with Avery just as they walk out the front door.

"Avery," I call out. "How did you guys get here?"

"We walked, it's not far."

"Okay. Well, I'm going to walk you home then."

"No, we're fine thanks." She tries to brush me off.

"Listen, my momma raised me right, and after what just happened, I'd feel a lot better knowing you made it home safe."

Avery gives me the side eye and has a silent conversation with Kelsey.

Finally, Kelsey turns to me. "Okay, handsome."

"Ignore her, she flirts with anything with a pulse," Avery jokes as she crosses her arms over her stomach and falls into step beside me. We walk in silence a bit and I walk a bit slower than normal not wanting the night to be over.

"The whole team knew, didn't they?" Avery finally breaks the silence in a voice barely above a whisper.

"Yes." She doesn't know I'm Titan, but I know, and I made a promise to be honest with her and I will keep it.

"Wow, it really is bros before hoes." She gives a fake laugh.

"You are the furthest thing from a ho," I state quietly.

"Well, you get the saying. I warned you about jocks," Kelsey singsongs, skipping beside me.

It causes me to flinch. "We aren't all like that."

"Right." Avery snorts. "And I shit rainbows. I see the girls all over you, too. Hell, they were even all over that Mick guy."

"Oh my god." Kelsey laughs. "He's so gross! Like, does he even know what soap is?"

Both girls laugh and I can't help but smile. I've questioned that a few times myself too, but he's a good player.

"Anything for a meal ticket, I guess." Kelsey skips off ahead of us a bit.

"Thanks for walking us home, I really appreciate it. You're one of the good ones, don't let them corrupt you," Avery says, her voice low.

The compliment warms my heart, and makes it race at the same time. I just wish she believed it enough to give me a chance, but if her conversation about jocks tonight is any indication, Kyle might have ruined that for her. I know she won't be wanting to date for a while, but I hope I have a chance when she is ready.

I smile at her. "He was never good enough for you anyway. A lot of us thought that."

She smiles back at me. "Well, I still know enough about him. He'd be stupid to mess with me again."

"I got pictures too," Kelsey chimes in, waving her phone in the air.

"What?" Avery asks, sounding as confused as I am.

"I got pictures of him with the girls before he jumped up. And of him grabbing you, in case we will need them."

"Nah, one call to the coach, and I could get him kicked off the team." Avery shakes her head.

"Not just for that, though," I say.

"No, not for that, but for what else I know. But I won't say anything as long as he leaves me alone."

I nod my head. "He gives you any trouble, let me know."

"Thanks." She starts up the steps to her building but stops and turns around. "Thank you again, for walking us home."

"You're welcome, now go get some sleep. Things will look better tomorrow."

She smiles and heads inside. I decide to head up to my room instead of rejoining the party once I get back to the house. Even though I know I won't be getting to sleep any time soon with how loud it is.

Me: You awake?

Avery: I have a better chance of seeing a unicorn than sleeping right now, Titan.

Me: I saw what happened.

Avery: Yeah, can't say I'm surprised. I had an inkling after I saw a hickey on him last week. I know I should have dealt with it then. Still, I'm relieved that it's over now. My roommate was quick to break out the wine in celebration as she calls it.

I wish I knew a way to help her and lighten the load on her shoulders, she should be enjoying this time of her life.

Me: Did I hear you call him out on his dick size?

Avery: Yeah, he couldn't even use it.

My heart starts to race, while I don't like the idea of Avery with Kyle. I do like the thought of Avery.

Me: Really?

Avery: Yeah, he never got me off. Can you blame me for not caring now it's over?

I take a deep breath and rub my hand over my face. I'm hard as a rock as I lie in bed and think about Avery getting off. Of course, I'm picturing her with me, which doesn't help to soften my dick in any way.

I know she's been drinking, so I should let it be, but a part of me wants to see where the conversation goes too.

Me: Wow, if you were my girl you'd get off before me every time, and always more than me.

I hesitate for only a second before sending. It's the truth, I'd treat her so good if she would only give me the chance.

Avery: That's the dream, but I don't know if guys like that really exist.

Me: We do. We just need to be given a chance.

Avery: Well, I don't have the time to date right now, or the trust, if I'm honest.

There it is, I know I will have an uphill battle to prove to her I am worth taking the chance on. I plan to make that climb though, because I know she's worth fighting for.

Me: Well, for the right guy, dating won't feel like such a chore.

Avery: I guess. Titan, do you have a girlfriend?

Does she really think I'd be texting her like this if I did? I guess I have more of an uphill battle than I thought. At least I can soothe a few her fears now.

Me: No, I haven't since high school.
Avery: Why?
Me: I don't think you want my answer.
Avery: No lies, right, Titan? Always honest.
Me: I'd never lie to you.
Avery: Then why?

I can't lie to her, I promised her I wouldn't, but at the same time, I don't feel like I can answer this question either. She is hurt and vulnerable right now and I think what I might say is the last thing she needs. But then, maybe this is also the perfect time to build trust with her too.

Me: Because I've been waiting for you.

When she doesn't respond I send another text.

Me: Are you mad?
Avery: Why would I be mad?
Me: Because I was the one who told you about Kyle.
Avery: A whole football team knew and kept it from me. So no, I'm not mad. I'm

thankful. Though if I'd have listened to my gut, I'd have done something about it before. I saw the hickeys; I could have confronted him.

Me: I'm sorry.

Avery: It's not your fault, but I am going to try to get some sleep now. Thank you, Titan.

Me: Goodnight, beautiful.

I set my phone down and images of Avery from tonight fill my head. She didn't dress up for the party but even in her shorts and a loose shirt with her wavy blond hair flowing down her back, she still looked like the goddess I thought she was the first time I saw her.

Combine that visual with our conversation about her not getting off and it's more than I can take. I reach my hand into my pants and pull out my cock. I close my eyes and picture Avery slowly stripping her out of those cut-off shorts.

I stroke my cock and think about her lying in my bed wearing nothing but black lace underwear, her golden hair fanned out around her. Her tan skin, soft and silky against my sheets.

Come starts to leak from my tip, so I spread it down my shaft and picture taking off Avery's bra and her luscious breasts bouncing out before I lean down and suck them into my mouth. Her back arches and I trail kisses to the top of her panties, then slowly pull them over her hips and down her legs, exposing her pink pussy.

The thought of Avery naked and laid out on my bed is enough to send me over the edge and hot come lands on my belly, causing me to groan. I take a minute to commit the image of a naked Avery lying on my bed to memory before getting up to clean myself off.

I'm just getting dressed again when there is a pounding on my door.

"Bolt, you coming down to enjoy the party? Some girls are asking about you!"

Kyle.

I open the door and take in the two girls from earlier on the back porch still hanging on him.

"No, I've got a headache I'm trying to shake before practice tomorrow."

"Man! They say an orgasm is the best headache cure."

I'm sure he'd say an orgasm cures anything, and he'd believe it.

"Thanks, but I'm going to lie down. Have fun, man."

"Alright, I'm sure I can please your lady friends for the night."

I shut the door before he can see me cringe, and check to make sure it's locked. He bounced back pretty fast; I can just hope Avery will as well.

Chapter 4

Avery

I walk in the door after my last class and Kelsey greets me with a double chocolate Oreo cupcake from the bakery just outside of campus.

"What did you do?" I ask her. I know this is either a bribe or an 'I'm sorry I destroyed your favorite shirt' cupcake.

"Well, it's been a week since the football party."

"Yes."

"You're still talking to Titan every day, right?"

"Yes."

"I think we should go to the football game tonight."

"Kelsey, I rarely went to the games when I was dating a football player!"

"I know, but I think this would be a good way to maybe flush out who Titan is!"

She thrusts the cupcake in my direction. I take it and plop down on the couch.

"Let me hear whatever plan you've already built up in your head," I say as I dig into the cupcake.

She sits down next to me and claps her hands excitedly.

"So, we go to the game and hold up spirit signs, but with Titan's name on it. We watch and see how the guys react to seeing them. Anyone thrown off by it gets added to our shortlist."

"I don't have a shortlist."

"Well, I have one."

"You do?! Who's on it?"

"Agree to go with me and I'll tell you."

I sigh. "Okay, I'll go, but I won't wear any guy's number or name on me, other than Titan's name on the signs."

"Deal," she squeals.

"Now, tell me who is on your list..."

"I just started it, so no one yet!" She jumps up and runs to her room to get ready.

"Not fair!" I call out after her.

"You didn't ask if anyone was on it, totally fair! Make sure to wear school colors!"

I dress in my Mountain Gap University shirt. School colors are similar to the Tennessee Titan colors, navy blue, and white. With it being a home game, the guys will be in their dark blue uniforms, which are my favorite.

My phone pings as I am doing my hair.

Titan: Will you be at the game tonight?"

"Kelsey!" I yell across the hall. "Titan wants to know if we will be at the game!"

"Tell him no, you are studying! We want him surprised that you're there!"

Me: No, I have some studying to catch up on.

Titan: A night at the football game makes a great study break.

Me: Not for me. I have a paper to finish. But good luck!

Titan: Okay, get your paper done and I will work on my bribing skills for the next home game.

Me: Deal.

"Come on, slowpoke, we need to make signs. I got the supplies before you came home."

Of course, she did. I add the last bit of curl to my hair, and mist some hair spray, and touch up my mascara before heading out to the living room.

"Does this outfit appease, my lady?" I gave a small curtsey as I enter the room.

"It does. Now grab a marker."

An hour later we are in line to get corn dogs and nachos because I have yet to have sucky food at this school, even the fries can be considered gourmet with the seasoning they put on them.

Food in hand, Kelsey smiles. "Come on, I got us some good seats!"

"How?"

"Well, a guy from my microbiology class asked me out, I suggested the game because you and I were going. He agreed and came early to get us seats. He's a swimmer!"

"So, this wasn't really about Titan?"

"Oh no, I had already planned to drag you here. It's just nice to have someone get us seats."

I roll my eyes. Kelsey is a huge flirt, she dates a lot, but doesn't sleep around. Since I'd known her, I only know of two guys she has slept with and she was in more of a serious relationship with them. Her motto is 'You have to date a lot of Mr. Wrongs to find Mr. Right.'. She has fun doing it, so it seems to work for her.

"Hey, Chris!"

"Kelsey!" He takes the nachos from her as we sit down.

"This is Avery," Kelsey says as she sits next to him. "Avery, this is Chris, he's on the swim team."

"Hi, Avery," he nods his head to me.

He isn't bad looking, he has the typical swimmer's body; lean and fit. He's not really my type. His blond hair is short, and every hair is in place. He seems like a nice enough guy though.

"What's with the posters?" Chris asks.

"Oh, it's an inside joke for a friend of Avery's." Kelsey shrugs and winks at me.

As the teams come out to the field, Kelsey pulls me up and we hold up our signs. A few guys look our way, but no one seems surprised.

"So, who's on your list now?"

"Mick, Sean, Denver, Derick, and whoever number twelve is... I forget."

I shake my head and sit down and as we eat, I find myself enjoying the game. By half time we are up by seven points, and the teams head to the locker rooms for a break. The southern summer heat is no joke.

A few minutes later my phone goes off.

Titan: Thought you couldn't make the game?

Me: So, you saw my signs...

Titan: I did, and I like you holding signs for me. Would be better if you were wearing my number.

Me: Well, if I knew your number, I could wear it.

Titan: Then I wouldn't be Titan anymore, plus I don't think you are ready to find out who I am. You and Kyle just broke up, it's better this way.

I do like things the way they are. I do want to know who Titan is, but I'm worried knowing will kill things. He's easy to talk to like this. I feel like I can be more myself because there is no one to face in the light of day.

Me: Kelsey has a shortlist of who she thinks you are.
Titan: Yeah? Pick one off her list, if you are right, I'll tell you after the game. You will have to come to another game to get another guess. See you on the field.

I show the text to Kelsey and watch the evil, *I have a plan* smile I know so well cross her face.
"Okay, strategy. Let's watch them as they come out on the field again and then we will decide."
I agree. I have no idea who it is. I guess I just don't want it to be Mick.
"I'm going to guess Mick cause if it is him, I want to end this now," I say.

"Oh gross, yeah make sure it isn't Mick."

Me: Are you Mick?

"Oh, and we get another guess next game... that gives us time to strategize," she says, narrowing her eyes and thinking deeply.

"Kels, the next two games are away games."

"Oh, that sucks. Then you need to get more info from him so we can make an informed guess."

The rest of the game seems to fly by. Mountain Gap takes home the win by fourteen points thanks to Denver and how fast he is. We run into some of Kelsey's friends as we're leaving, so by the time we head out most of the crowd is gone and the players are heading to their cars.

"A-VER-Y!" Derick calls out. I always liked him, he was nice when Kyle and I hung out with him. He's a big flirt and always treats you like you're his best friend but he's innocent enough. Kelsey elbows me and I turn to say hi and stop when I see Denver is with him.

"Hey Derick, Denver," I nod and smile at him

"Hey, girl. You coming to the party tonight?" Derick asks.

"No, the game was enough fun for me."

"Come on, Avery, just for a bit," Kelsey begs.

"No, really, I'm done for the night. I'm sure Derick or Denver would be happy to have you go with them."

"No, I'll go home with you," she mumbles. "It was a lot of work just to get you out to the game. I will have to up my bribing skills next time to include the party."

"Aw, next time?" Derick asks with a fake pout. He's a true player, but a nice guy who is honest about it all and upfront.

"Maybe." I smile at him as I turn to head back.

"Avery?" Denver smirks.

"Yeah?"

"Titan said to tell you, wrong guess."

Kelsey's eyes go big. "Thank god, that would be weird." She loops her arm through mine. "Okay, home we go. We need to make our list."

She starts pulling me away, but my eyes never leave Denver's as I take in the smirk on his face and the twinkle in his eye.

Chapter 5

Avery

The next few weeks are filled with classes, work, and daily texts from Titan. We talk about anything and everything. He tells me about growing up with a single mom and how he got into football. I tell him about my parents and how they are traveling now that they are empty nesters.

He asks about Nashville, we talk about our favorite things to do around campus, our classes, and even stay in to watch a few movies together, texting the whole time.

Kelsey and I went to another home game and got another guess. She guessed Derick and we got a no. Halloween passed and we skipped the football Halloween party this year for the baseball player's party since Kelsey was dating one of the guys there. He was a horrible dancer, so Halloween ended that short-lived fling.

Titan gave me crap for a week about us ditching the football party for the baseball one and said how he would have danced with me. When I pointed out that it would've meant I'd find out who he was, he said he would have had on a mask.

I joked and said I doubted he missed me as he had plenty of other girls to dance with. That seems to make him mad, but he finally admitted he didn't even go down to the party. Parties aren't really his thing, apparently.

Today I am working at the coffee shop and it's slow due to most people being in class. When Kyle walks in he looks a bit shy but walks up to the counter.

"Hey, Avery, can we talk a minute?"

"I'm at work, as you can see, but you can have until the next customer comes in." I keep my voice flat and cold.

He nods and looks at the door and then back at me "Listen, I'm sorry about that night at the party. I was drunk and no matter what happened I shouldn't have put my hands on you. I'm sorry I hurt you. I know I should have broken it off a while ago, but I liked hanging out with you."

I sigh. "If you had broken it off before you cheated, we could have stayed friends and we could have kept hanging out. Now I don't even want to be around you."

He nods. "I know and I don't blame you."

My phone goes off and I glance down at it.

Titan: So, the word is someone went to coach about what Kyle did to you at the party. He's benched for the next two games.

I roll my eyes and type out a quick response.

Me: That would be why he is here now apologizing.

"Who's that?" Kyle asks., and I have to bite my tongue, so I don't tell him to get out.

"Kyle, you lost the right to ask me that, remember?"

"Sorry. I just wanted to come and say I was sorry, and I was stupid. I never meant to hurt you and I just want you to be happy. I mean that, Avery."

I don't want to hold a grudge. I've never been one to put energy into hating. Kyle sounds like he means it, but knowing he's benched I am willing to bet the coach made him come and apologize and smooth things over, so I don't cause problems for the team. Though I have to wonder why the team is just now finding out about this, it's been almost a month.

My phone goes off again, but I ignore it this time. I decide to let him off the hook and keep things civil.

"Thank you, Kyle."

He nods then looks at me again. "Can I ask you a question?"

"Sure, and I might even answer it."

"Did you really never... umm... you know with me?"

"No, I don't know Kyle." I know what he wants to know, but I want to make him sweat it out a bit more.

My phone goes off, again, and again, I still ignore it.

He looks a bit embarrassed. "Get off."

"Oh. Yeah, that part was true."

Red stains his cheeks and I almost feel sorry for him. Almost.

"Well, I need to get back to the gym, I'm supposed to weight train with Sean this afternoon."

"Bye, Kyle."

"Bye, Avery."

I watch him walk out the door and my phone goes off again.

Titan: What is he saying?

Titan: Avery, you okay?

Titan: You need me to come down and get him to leave?

Titan: Please, just let me know you're okay.

Me: If I said yes, I want you to make him leave, it would out your secret identity.

Titan: It would be worth it to make sure you're okay. I don't trust him off the field.

Yeah well, I don't know how you can trust him on the field either. I shake my head and take a deep breath, I need to let this all go.

Me: I'm fine. He apologized, we talked for a minute and he just left.
Titan: Sure you're okay?

I snap a quick picture of me smiling in the empty coffee shop and before I can think better, I attach it to my next text.

Me: Promise. See, all in one piece and he's gone. You really would have shown up?

It's a few minutes before his next text comes in.

Titan: Yes. I would have shown up. Damn, you're beautiful, Avery.

Heat creeps up my neck and I rub a hand across my forehead. When was the last time a guy made me *feel* beautiful?

Me: Thank you, Titan.

Things pick up again at the shop and in the last thirty minutes of my shift I'm cleaning up and restocking when the door chime signals someone entered. When I come around the corner, Denver is at the counter, he smiles when he sees me.

"Hey, I just got done with class and need a pick me up."

I notice he is wearing a Tennessee Titans shirt.

Surely, he isn't Titan. Right?

He notices me staring at his shirt and smiles.

"Few of the guys and I went to Nashville and toured the stadium last spring break. We got to do some training with some of the players."

"That's pretty cool." I set down the box I had in my hand. "What can I get you?"

"A large coffee. Do you have any Thanksgiving plans?"

"Yeah, I'm heading home to Nashville. My parents are going to be home for Thanksgiving, but my mom is refusing to cook. She's ordered a ready done meal from Loveless Cafe this year. They plan to decorate for Christmas then they are off to some small town in Washington that has a huge Christmas event in December, and they will get home just in time to have Christmas with me." I hand Denver his coffee.

"They travel a lot?"

"Yeah, ever since I left for school. They only ever go home when I am. They have hit every state, most of the National Parks, and all but three countries in Europe. They are planning an Africa trip next year. It's all I've heard about."

"You travel a lot with them growing up?" he asks, leaning on the counter and taking a sip of his coffee.

"We did summer vacations to the National Parks, but that's really about it. What about you, any family vacations?"

"Once to Pensacola. My mom won tickets and we got a four-day weekend away down there. We spent it mostly at the beach. My mom got bit by a sand crab on the last day and it was enough to get us off the beach to check out the shops." He laughs.

I smile and start stocking things up.

"Did you hear Kyle got benched?"

"Yeah, he was in here earlier, he apologized, and we talked. It was good closure. I think he needed more than I did."

"Why do you say that?"

"He asked about a few of the comments I made that night. It was nice to see him humble and not his cocky self. Reminded me of the Kyle I used to know."

"Think you will give him another chance?" he asks hesitantly.

"Gosh, no. Cheating is a hard line with me. You don't get another chance after that."

"Same here." He gives me that crooked half smile all the girls melt over.

We chat a bit more about classes and finals before the door dings and a group of girls walk in.

"Well, good talking to you. See you in class." He gives me a wave and heads out.

I get home and Kelsey is waiting with another cupcake. "What do you want now?" I sigh but take the cupcake and head for the couch.

"So, this really hot guy asked me out in class today, he's a soccer player. I mentioned I needed to check with you because we usually hang out on Friday nights, and he suggested we double date with his buddy who is also on the soccer team."

"No way, Kelsey. I'm not ready to date."

"I told him that you just broke up with Kyle and that he had cheated so you weren't ready to date. He said it was perfect because his friend just got dumped and isn't really wanting to date. It would be like you two are there as friends with us, who are friends who happen to be on a date," she says this at a hundred miles an hour and I can hardly keep up.

"Kelsey, my head hurts just trying to follow that logic."

"Please, please, please, Avery."

"This Friday?"

"No, it's the Friday after Thanksgiving break."

I sigh. "It's going to take more than a cupcake for this one."

"My mom will be here that weekend and she promised to make her fried chicken and honey biscuits for you."

Ugh, her mom's fried chicken and biscuits are my weakness. She knows I will do just about anything for them.

"Fine, but you better have her make extras so I can have lunches for a week!"

"Deal!"

Chapter 6

Denver

I wake up and hear my mom moving around in the kitchen. I drove home yesterday to spend Thanksgiving weekend with her. Even though it's just the two of us, she insists on cooking a proper meal with the works.

Yesterday she cooked both pumpkin and apple pie for dessert and I know she was up at the crack of dawn to start the turkey. Whatever turkey we don't eat, I'll help her pull off the bones and she will freeze it and eat off it for weeks.

"Hey, Mom," I say as I shuffle my way into the kitchen for some coffee.

"Hey, baby, I'm just about to put this bird in the oven but it's heavy. Will you lift it in for me?"

"Of course. You know this one is about double the size of last year's turkey, right?"

"I know but Clint gave out some turkeys at work and insisted I have this one, he remembers how much he ate at your age. He also gave me a $50 grocery gift card to cover the rest. Isn't that just sweet of him? I really love working there."

She has had this job as Clint's assistant for about ten years now, and Clint always rewards his loyal, hardworking employees. The longer Mom works there the more he does for her.

When he found out she was having to work nights to pay for my football stuff in high school, he gave her a raise and a trial promotion taking on more work than just his secretary. He offered her overtime as it came up, just so she wouldn't have to work two jobs and would be able to go to all my games.

My mom worked hard, and he promoted her to his assistant a few years back which is how she is able to afford the house she is in now.

Once the bird is in the oven, Mom pulls out the cinnamon rolls she made earlier, and we sit at the table to eat breakfast.

"So, last I heard Avery broke up with Kyle and you were texting with her. How're things going now?"

Yeah, my mom is also my best friend. I don't keep secrets from her, either. She knows about Avery and she felt so guilty about pulling me away from her at that party all those years ago, but I assured her I'd have felt guiltier if she hadn't.

"We've been texting every day, which reminds me..." I pull my cell out of my pocket and fire off a quick text to Avery.

Me: Good morning, beautiful. Happy Thanksgiving.

My mom smiles. "So romantic, Den."

"We're getting to know each other, and she has shown up for more games since she broke up with Kyle than the whole time they were dating."

"Do you think Kyle will cause any problems when you two finally get together?"

I sigh. "If we get together, I'm pretty sure he will." I love how optimistic my mom is, but it's hard when I know how little Avery trusts football players right now.

As we finish breakfast Mom tells me about what is going on at work. I take both our dishes to the sink then turn back to face her.

"I'll be back for lunch Mom. I promised Mrs. Gardner and Mr. McLean I'd mow their yards this morning."

"Okay, I was thinking some soup for lunch and then we can eat dinner a bit early."

"Sounds perfect."

While I mow my mom's neighbors' yards and use the weed eater to get the edging, my mind is on Avery. She said her parents were coming home for Thanksgiving, but her mom wasn't cooking. She said she didn't care because it meant her mom could enjoy some game time with her and her dad.

I've enjoyed talking with her and I've been debating on when I should reveal who I am. The closer we get, the worse I feel that she doesn't know who I am.

Though she and Kelsey have a fun time guessing.

About a week ago they were drinking, and Kelsey decided to send a voice message over to me, asking for just one number for my jersey for a hint. I saved the message and have listened to Avery's laugh every night before bed.

I told them my jersey has the number 1 on it, which narrowed down their list to 5 people. Though Avery said Kelsey was second guessing herself and added two new people to it.

"Oh, Denver, the yard looks amazing," Mr. McLean says. "I hate to ask, but I need some help getting stuff out of the attic if you have a minute. My granddaughter is graduating high school this year and I'd like to pass on some things to her."

"Of course, Mr. McLean."

I check my phone before heading up.

Avery: Happy Thanksgiving to you too. Favorite Thanksgiving dish?

And just like that, we are back to our routine of asking question after question all day. It takes me thirty minutes to find the boxes Mr. McLean is looking for and he's paid me double for the lawn.

When I try to refuse, he gets stern with me.

"Now listen, young man. I know you give this money to your mom. She is a sweet lady and how you've turned out is a testament of what an amazing mother she is. You give that money to her, and don't complain."

"Yes, sir, thank you."

I get home, shower, and get ready to spend the afternoon with my mom. I look for her purse which she normally keeps by the door to slip the money in, but she just smirks.

"Looking for something?"

I sigh. "Why do you make this so hard on me?"

"Because I wish you would take that money and use it at school. I insist this time."

"If you're so worried, put in with the allowance you insist on putting in my account each month."

"Of which you don't use. I know it's not much, but I want you to go out and have fun, experience college. You only get to do this once."

"I have no one to spend it on." I shrug.

"When Avery is ready, you'll have someone to spend it on." She holds out her hand and I put the money in it.

"I thought you only had two yards?"

"I did, but Mr. McLean had some other work around the house for me and got mad when I tried to refuse the money."

She rolls her eyes and shakes her head lightly, amazed at the kindness of some people. We watch the end of the Thanksgiving Day parade and start on our annual Santa Claus movies. She says it's her favorite way to start off Christmas. Tomorrow we will spend the day decorating the house, inside and out.

I spend the day texting with Avery and Mom asks me about school and my games. She can't make it to every one, but she watches them all even if she has to record and watch them later. Some nights she has called at 1 a.m. when she finishes watching just to congratulate me on a win and talk about the game.

I help her make the sides and we sit down for dinner. We take time to pray and say what we are thankful for every year. Mom always goes first.

"I am thankful for you and the chance you have to play football. That you are healthy and happy, and you are mine. I am thankful for my job and the raise I got last month. The food on the table and the roof over my head."

She squeezes my hand and I know it's my turn. The last few years what I'm thankful for is pretty much the same. This year there is only one difference.

"I'm thankful for you, Mom. For the sacrifices you made for me growing up so I can play football and be here today. I'm thankful for your love, support, and guidance. This year I am thankful Avery broke up with Kyle and that she is now happy. I am thankful she is in my life, any way I can have her, and I'm thankful she is healthy."

If the guys could hear me, I'm sure they'd revoke my man card with how sappy I am. We dig in and about halfway through dinner, someone knocks on the door. I get up to answer thinking it's one of the neighbors, only to find my piece-of-shit father on the other side. How has he tracked her down?

This is the first time I've seen him since my senior year of high school and he looks like shit, he's thin and looks like he hasn't slept in days. I go to close the door in his face without a word, but he takes me by surprise by kicking it open and walking in. I didn't expect him to be that strong.

"Go home, you weren't invited," I grit out. I have no desire to see this man I share DNA with. The last thing I want is for my mom to know he's here.

"What are you doing here, Ted?" Mom asks, her voice flat.

I sigh of course my mom wouldn't wait at the table for me. I don't trust him, if he's here he wants something.

"It's Thanksgiving, and this is my boy. I'm here for Thanksgiving dinner."

"No one invited you," I say through, trying to hold back the rage boiling inside me. "You aren't welcome here; we aren't family." I stand protectively between him and my mom.

"The hell we ain't, it's half my blood in your veins that makes you so great at football... you owe me." He smirks.

He can't be serious; he thinks a little DNA from someone who has no athletic talent got me to where I am?

"I'm good at football because I busted my ass, not because of anything you did. You did nothing," My voice raises with each word.

"Ahhh, that's not how I see it. You owe me, so why don't you sign some of this stuff here in my car so I can sell it and we can call it even."

Money. Of course, he's here for money. I'm surprised he hasn't just tried to walk out with our TV like the last time I saw him. I clench my fists. I'd love nothing more than to land a good punch and feel the satisfying crunch of breaking his nose, but I know that would make headlines and the coach would bench me. I take a deep breath before responding.

"Why would I do that? You owe Mom thousands in backdated child support." I fail to keep the anger out of my voice.

"You're eighteen. I owe her nothing." He laughs thinking he's won this one.

"Not according to the government. That doesn't go away, she raised me you didn't pay. You still owe her. Now get out before I call the cops, I'm sure you have a warrant out based on the child support alone."

"I'm your father, family, you don't treat family like this." He takes a step forward, but I don't back down. I'm not a small scared kid anymore. I know I can take him, and I won't let him try to push Mom or me around anymore.

"I don't have a father. You're a piece of shit that I sadly share DNA with. Get. Out. Now."

"You teach him this crap, Gina?"

"No, he learned it on his own last time you tried to scam him," my mom snaps back.

I pull out my cell phone and get ready to hit the call button.

"I'm going. I'm going." He watches to make sure I don't hit dial.

"You still owe me, boy." He says over his shoulder as he walks down the steps.

"I owe you a trip to the ER if you show up here again!" I yell after him

I watch him drive away, but unease still fills my gut. My mom places a hand on my shoulder in an attempt to calm me down.

"I don't know how he found you, but I don't like him knowing where you live," I say as I watch him drive away.

I try to calm down by making plans to secure her house better this weekend. I can add a few more locks to the doors at the very least.

"I don't know either. But I doubt he shows up again anytime soon." There's a shake in her voice and I'm not sure who she is trying to convince.

"You let me know if he does." I look over at her. She meets my eyes and doesn't break eye contact as she stares at me for a moment before nodding.

"I will now let's eat. We won't let that man ruin our dinner."

Chapter 7

Avery

I hate blind dates, and no matter how Kelsey tries to spin it, that's what this is. I don't want to be on this date, so I am not dressing up. Jeans and a nice shirt, I straighten my hair toss on a bit of make-up, and I'm done.

I haven't heard from Titan since this morning, he had some football meetings and training and he told me he would be busy.

We get to the restaurant early, so we get a seat and I make Kelsey buy me a glass of wine. I think I'm going to need it.

Titan: Working tonight?
Me: No, I had an early shift.
Titan: So, what are you up to tonight?
Me: Kelsey dragged me on a blind date.

"Please tell me you aren't going to be texting with Titan all night," Kelsey says, rolling her eyes. "Please give this guy a chance."

"I knew this was a set-up! And the guys aren't here yet, Titan is, so he wins my attention."

She rolls her eyes again and turns her attention back to her phone. Titan still hasn't answered so I sip my wine and check out the menu before my phone goes off again.

Titan: I didn't know you were ready to start dating again.

I can't help but smile and picture a big football player pouting right now.

Me: I wasn't, but she bribed me with her mom's famous fried chicken and honey biscuits. It's my weakness. She also had cupcakes. I blame the sugar coma.

Titan: Have fun.

Wow, Titan is never short with me like this. He always finds ways to keep me talking. Then it hits me, and I smile.

Me: Why, Titan, are you jealous?
Titan: Yes.
Me: Honest and to the point, I like it.

Just then the guys show up.

"Avery, this is Ollie, my date, and this is Jeremy, your date."

Jeremy reaches out and shakes my hand, it's all very formal and awkward. As we sit, I take in Jeremy. He looks very much like a preppy jock, and so very much not my type. I like them more rugged, but I know I should give him a chance.

Kelsey and Ollie are already lost in conversation, so I offer Jeremy a smile. "I'm not a fan of blind dates, they can be a bit awkward."

"Yeah, this is my first blind date. Not that I'm ready to date again."

"I told Kelsey that too, but then she bribed me with her mom's cooking, and I couldn't say no."

"Ollie is doing my laundry for a month. Fair trade, I guess." He shrugs his shoulders.

My phone goes off and I ignore it and try to talk to Jeremy. He's really smart and plays soccer, but he gives me weird looks when I make a joke. I've come to the conclusion he's just boring. Not a single piece of his dark blond hair is out of place, he's perfectly clean-shaven and just... well... boring.

When Ollie and Jeremy start telling a story about a recent game, I check my phone.

>**Titan:** Is he there?
>**Titan:** Please tell me he's ugly.
>**Titan:** Boring?
>**Titan:** Need an SOS call?

I smile at that. I'm sure he is pacing the room right now and I wish I had a face to put with the image.

"Everything okay?" Jeremy asks.

"Oh yeah, just someone checking in because they haven't heard from me in a while. Let me tell them I'm fine."

Kelsey gives me a look that says she can see right through me; she knows I'm texting Titan.

Me: He's here. He's not bad looking but he isn't my type. He's a soccer player and is very boring. He also seems annoyed by my jokes.

Titan responds almost instantly so I have to wonder if he isn't staring at his phone waiting for my text.

Titan: Need an SOS call?
Me: No, I need fried chicken.
Titan: I can come to get you right now and I will take you to the best fried chicken you have ever eaten. Promise. It's award winning.
Me: You that desperate to get me away from my date?
Titan: Yes.

I glance up at Jeremy who is also on his phone, so I text back.

Me: Why?
Titan: If I had known you were ready to date, I'd have asked you out. I should be the one sitting there not Mr. Boring Jock.

Me: I will finally find out who you are?
Titan: Yes.

I smile. If I had known a date was all it would take for Titan to reveal himself, I might have done it sooner. I look over at Kelsey and she is all wrapped up in Ollie and Jeremy is checking out one of the waitresses.

Me: Okay. We are at the Grill.
Titan: See you soon, Coffee Girl.

I pick up a roll and try to eat it, but my appetite is gone. I'm debating if I should leave before Titan gets here. What if finding out who he is ruins everything? This is such a big step. I shouldn't have made such a rash decision.

I bite my lip and wonder if it's too late to tell him I've changed my mind. I smooth down my shirt and shift in my seat just as someone approaches the table.

Chapter 8

Denver

I walk into The Grill and it's easy to spot Avery with her gorgeous blond hair. Although, I'm sure I could spot her in any crowd. As I walk up to the table, my heart is racing. Maybe I didn't think this through properly. But when her date starts checking out the waitress, I know she deserves better and I need to get her out of there.

When I stop by the side of the table, Avery looks up at me and bites her bottom lip, tilting her head to the side like she wants to question why I'm here. I just wink at her and smile.

"I was told you were promised some fried chicken?"

Her jaw drops and the guy across from her looks confused. I can't blame him, I doubt he was expecting some football player to come in and steal his girl. Not that she was ever his to begin with.

I hold out my hand to Avery, praying she takes it and leaves with me. When she laughs and places her hand in mine, the sparks that flickered during our one and only kiss are still as strong as ever. Everything feels right at this moment.

She stands up and turns to her date. "Sorry, but I don't think this is going to work." She catches Kelsey's eye and shrugs her shoulders. "I apparently have a date with Titan."

Hell yeah, she does. Watching the shock cross Kelsey's face is worth ruining this set-up for. I take her hand, turning and leading her out, with both of us trying to contain our nervous, excited giggles. I open her door to my truck, sweeping my hand out in a gesture for her to get in, before I jog to the other side and get myself.

She turns to face me, her eyes wide. "You're really Titan?"

The question in her voice has me a little nervous, was she hoping I was someone else?

"Surprised?"

"Shocked as hell."

I offer her a small smile, but my nerves have now hit me full force as I start to drive.

She places her hand on my arm. "I'm glad it's you."

I smile big this time. We head out of the city and she is looking out the window as the town turns into farmland. I know she is trying to process all the texting and everything we've spoken about, consolidating it with me and not some mystery man.

"Where are we going?"

"You'll see, it is a little bit of a drive."

"Everything you said when we were texting..."

"All of it true, it was one hundred percent me, unfiltered. Avery, I promised you that and I meant it."

We finally pull up to my mom's neighborhood. It's not the best, but it's not the worst. I made sure she was safe. When I called her and asked if she would make fried chicken and told her I had someone I wanted her to meet, she didn't even care that it was late notice. She was so excited and seemed to know right off the bat it was Avery.

When we park, I walk around and help Avery out as my mom steps out onto the porch.

"Hey, Mom, this is Avery," I say as she wraps me in a huge hug.

"I love your last-minute visits, baby."

Mom turns to Avery and says, "Well, aren't you the sweetest thing!" and then wraps her in a huge hug too.

Even though my mom knows about Avery, she doesn't let on how much she knows.

"Come in, come in. Dinner is almost ready. I was so excited when you called, I even made dessert."

"Thanks, Mom."

"You made your mom cook?" Avery asks, shaking her head, but she has a huge smile on her face.

"Oh, trust me, I'm happy to do it. I've heard so much about you, so him bringing you home, I'd cook a feast."

"My mom makes the best fried chicken. I'm willing to bet it's better than Kelsey's mom's. She's won a few awards for it."

Avery's eyes light up. "Really?"

"Really." I pull out her chair for her to sit and then pull out my mom's.

"Thank you, baby," Mom says, taking my hand and Avery's to say grace. Getting to hold Avery's hand, even across the table is all I was able to concentrate on, so much so that I don't hear a word of mom's prayer until she says Amen.

I watch Avery dig into my mom's fried chicken, and when she closes her eyes and lets out a soft moan, I'm instantly hard and wish she was making those sounds for me.

I have to close my eyes and think of gross athletes' foot to get my cock to go down. Sitting next to my mother is not the place to be sporting a hard on.

"This really is the best fried chicken I think I've ever had." Avery smiles and then digs in again.

"Worth ditching soccer man for?"

She smiles. "Yes, definitely."

"I feel like there is a story there." Mom laughs.

Avery tells my mom about her night before I rescued her, how Kelsey bribed her to do this blind date and how boring the guy was. By the end of her story, my mom is laughing, and I can't help but smile too.

I'm still a bit nervous about how this dinner will go. I never expected this to be my first date with Avery, but seeing her face light up over the food, I know I've made the right choice.

I love seeing Avery get along with my mom. I haven't brought a girl home since high school, and when I called earlier to ask my mom about bringing Avery by, well, I haven't heard her that excited in a long time.

They are getting along great and that is a huge deal to me since my mom is the most important woman in my life. I know

I couldn't be with someone who didn't get along with her.

"Where does your family live?" Mom asks her while passing her more chicken.

"Nashville. Actually, I have to head home winter break; I've got to get my grandma's house taken care of."

"What do you mean?" my mom asks. I'm interested as well. She hasn't mentioned this even texting me as Titan.

"Well, over the summer my grandma passed. She left me the house and everything in it. It's been paid off for a long time and with my parents now being empty nesters, they want to travel. They don't need the house or the money, so they suggested, and my grandparents agreed, to leave it all to me. My parents went in and took what they wanted, mostly mementos, photos and such."

"What do you plan to do with it?"

She smiles at my mom. "My parents have been helping me sort through things, but the plan right now is to go back and go through the stuff in the house. I need to see what to keep, what to get rid of, and make a list of the repairs and stuff needing to be done. I'm thinking of renting it out until I am done with school. It's in good shape. Grandma started to remodel it after Grandpa died, so the bathrooms and kitchen are done, and those are the hard rooms. My parents are letting me store everything I'm keeping in their basement to clear the house out. I spent some time there this summer, but I wasn't ready to get rid of anything."

Mom places her hand on Avery's arm. "Are you ready to now?"

"I don't know." She looks down at her hands thoughtfully then back up to my mom. "I think so. There are some things I want. My grandparents had a few collections and I'd like to keep a few items. I've been going over what is in the house in my head I know the place inside and out, I practically grew up there. I know what furniture I want to keep and what I plan to sell. Many are antiques..." She laughs. "A few just give me the creeps and I want gone sooner rather than later."

Mom and I both laugh at that.

"Mom had this painting while I was growing up that she loved," I say. "But I swear it was staring at me and it creeped me out so bad I refused to be in the house alone at one point."

Mom giggles. "Yes, then when you turned fifteen, it mysteriously went missing."

"It may or may not have been subject to an accidentally-on-purpose accident and given a proper burial."

"Denver!"

"Sorry, Mom, but that painting really was horrible."

Mom grins and shakes her head, but Avery is laughing and any scolding I might get from my mom later over that painting is worth it.

"I was making weekend trips home for a bit just going through things and prepping myself to move stuff. But my grades started to slip, and I made the choice to wait until winter break." Avery offers a sad smile.

"That's why you were so tired?" I ask.

"Yeah. Kyle never wanted to come and help, but then couldn't understand why I couldn't hang out on weekends. I ended up spending less time at the house than I wanted."

I nod my head but see my mom squeeze her hand. "If you need extra hands to help, we'd be more than willing to. I have those two weeks of Christmas break off of work."

"Oh no, it's Christmas, you're supposed to spend it together, you don't want to spend it with me going through an old home."

"It's just the two of us and we offered, plus, I want Mom to see Nashville and get to know the area a bit."

I can see her thinking while she eats her biscuit and I really do want her to say yes. Spending two weeks with Avery would be an amazing way to spend Christmas.

"How good are you with a paintbrush?" she asks, and me and Mom look at each other and grin.

"We're pros," my mom answers.

"I'd like the company. My parents don't get in until Christmas Eve, then they leave two days later to go visit my mom's family."

"They aren't helping?" I'm a bit shocked that they would leave her to do all this herself.

"They offered, but I planned to have them help move furniture and then do the boxes myself. They always visit my mom's family this time of year and I didn't want them to change their plans. Plus, it lets me go at my own pace as I go through things. It took some convincing and a little white lie to get them to agree to not change their plans. The house is plenty big so you can stay with me. It's been closed up for a bit though, so be warned."

"Oh, that doesn't scare us off." Mom waves her hand at Avery.

After dinner, Mom brings out dessert. She calls it an Oreo dirt pie. All I know is that it's amazing.

"Oh my gosh, Oreos are my weakness," Avery says as she stares at the dessert set down on the table. My mom serves us each a slice and I can't wait to dig in. Mom would only make this for special occasions growing up, but it's always been my favorite.

"This is so addictive and one of my favorites," I say.

"It's really good," Avery agrees.

"Thanks, it's a family recipe." Mom smiles.

"You are an amazing cook. If I spend too much time around you, I'm going to gain fifty pounds." Avery laughs.

When we're both so stuffed, we can hardly move, I glance at the clock. "I hate to eat and run, Mom, but it's a long drive back to campus."

"Oh, I know, baby. I'm so excited you came out tonight. Avery, you are welcome back any time. Make plans with Denver, please, and we will be there to help you." Mom hugs Avery and then turns and hugs me. "Drive safe and shoot me a quick text to let me know you made it back ok."

"I promise. Love you, Mom."

"Love you too." She kisses my cheek and closes the door behind us.

Once in the car, Avery turns to me. "I like your mom."

"I can tell she liked you too."

"You guys really don't mind helping me out over Christmas break?"

"I promise we don't mind. I'd love to spend the break with you. It's just me and Mom so being around more people would be fun."

Her phone pings, and she starts texting.

"Everything okay?" I ask.

"Yeah, it's just Kelsey checking up on me."

We talk a bit about her family and her grandparents on the way home. When we get back to campus I pull up in front of her place and walk her to her door.

"Sorry again that your date was a dud. I hope I made up for it."

"It's okay I ended up on a much better date." She smiles and knowing that smile is for me sends my heart racing and makes my hands ache to reach out and touch her.

I can't stop the grin that takes over my face. "Well then, let's make it official."

I lean in and place my hand on her waist as she looks up at me and licks her lips. I slowly close the distance between us until my lips land on hers for the first time since that party.

The first kiss we shared was mind blowing and amazing, but this kiss tops it. My feelings for Avery have only grown the more I've gotten to know her. This is soul searing. I gently place my other hand behind her neck and pull her in close as she wraps her arms around my waist.

She opens her mouth and my tongue slowly explores hers as I take my time memorizing how her body feels pressed to mine, how her lips feel against mine, and how she feels in my arms. I rest my forehead on hers as I catch my breath and hold her in my arms, where she is supposed to be, and where I plan to keep her.

Chapter 9

Avery

My lips are still tingling from Denver's kiss on Friday night. I was up way later than I should have been every night this weekend thinking about that kiss and the fact that *he* is Titan. Since finding out, I've reread all our text messages, and looking back there are a few hints I missed.

He hasn't changed. I still get a good morning text from him every morning which makes me smile. Now it's Monday and I head out the door to go to class and Denver is there.

"May I have the honor of walking you to class?"

I can't help but laugh. "I'd like that."

"So, my mom called me almost as soon as I walked into my room demanding I bring you home again soon, and to make sure I get the plans for Christmas break. She's excited about it."

"Well if I'm honest, I'm excited for the company. I had planned to leave the Friday Christmas break starts. Will your finals be over then?"

"Yep, we're good to go." He gives me that smile of his that the girls all melt over it.

We walk into class together and I expect him to go to his normal seat upfront, but he follows me and sits next to me.

"What are you doing?"

"Sitting next to my girl. Is that okay?"

"Your girl?"

He laughs. "Well I'm hoping you will agree to be mine, so I'm going to treat you like you are and that starts with not hanging out with the Jersey Chasers."

Like he summoned them out of thin air, Sasha, the queen Jersey Chaser, stops by his seat.

"Denver, are you coming to sit with us?" she coos, pushing her overexposed chest toward him.

"Nope, I'm good here." Denver stares at me, ignoring her, and I don't think there is a girl on the planet who wouldn't be affected by having Denver's attention like this. My lips tingle remembering that kiss and I want to pull him in for another one.

"Well, when you get bored, you know where to find us." She gives what I'm sure she thinks is a sexy pout but looks more like she had bad lip fillers.

"Not going to happen." He leans into me, dismissing her, and he doesn't see the nasty look she gives me before heading to her seat with the other girls.

"Slow, Denver. Very slow," I whisper.

"Slow as you need. We can start with dinner on Saturday. You can bring Kelsey and her date, if it makes you feel better."

"I can do dinner, no Kelsey necessary, if you take me for tacos."

"Done."

"Not just any tacos, there's a food truck that makes the best street tacos, but we have to track them down."

"Derick has been talking about those tacos too, but I haven't tried them yet.

Now I really can't wait for Saturday. What are the chances I can get you to Friday's game?"

I just shake my head. He's working pretty hard for a player.

"Sweet girl..." the look he gives me has a hint of amusement in it. "Do you not remember me saying that I've been waiting for you?"

Shoot, I said the last part out loud.

"I'm just having a hard time connecting you and Titan into one in my head."

His face softens. "I get that. No lies, remember? Truth is, those girls annoy the shit out of me. Truth is, I haven't even kissed anyone or slept with anyone since our kiss freshman year. Truth is, I will wait as long as you need, just don't push me away."

I just shake my head. What can I even say to that? Thank you seems wildly inappropriate. I go for a subject change.

"If Kelsey can come with me, I'll be at the game on Friday."

***

Kelsey is beyond excited to go to the game with me and has even made posters for us.

I get home from class on Friday before her, and there is a boy with a box and a card with my name on it. He looks familiar but I don't remember his name.

"You're from the football team, right?" I ask.

"Um, yes, I'm Cory, I'm a freshman," he stammers and then shakes his head. "Denver asked me to give this to you. He has a meeting with coach."

"Thank you, Cory." I take the box and head inside before I open the card.

Avery,

I can't wait to see you at the game cheering for me, knowing it's me. Even more so I can't wait to see you at the game wearing my number.

This is for you, sweet girl. Wait for me after the game?

Denver

Inside is his jersey with his number 18 on it. I go get ready in a pair of jeans and his jersey, taking extra time to curl my hair and do my make-up. When I step out of my room Kelsey is already ready to go. I hadn't even heard her come home. I think she is more excited about the food than the game.

We get our food and head to the seats Denver got for us—front row, right by the team. As we sit down, Sasha and her other Jersey Chasers walk by.

"Enjoy him while you can. He's on a normal girl kick but he'll be tired of you soon and back in bed with me." Sasha smiles at me.

"Dream on," Kelsey says with a curl of her lip. "We can all see how disgusted he is when you touch him. Move on." Kelsey rolls her eyes at her and Sasha's face gets red as she stomps away.

"Don't think you should have done that," I sing song to her with a hint of amusement in my voice.

"I spoke the truth and we both know it. I'm not worried."

We watch the team come out and before everyone takes the field Denver runs up to the fence.

"I really like my number on you," he calls out to me.

"I like wearing it." I smile.

"Turn around, sweet girl, I want to see my name on you."

I turn slowly and pull my hair to the side for him.

He groans. "You are going to wait for me after the game, right?"

"Yeah, Kelsey is going to wait with me."

He raises his helmet to me and runs off to join his team. I watch with butterflies stirring in my tummy.

He scores several touchdowns and after each one he points to me in the crowd, while Kelsey and I yell and scream for him.

After the game, which we won, we stop for Kelsey to get a soft pretzel and then head to the door where he will be coming out. Of course, Sasha and the Jersey Chasers are already there and it's really hard not to tell they are talking about us.

Denver walks out, freshly showered and in jeans and a T-shirt. His eyes lock with mine, and his smile lights up his face.

Sasha steps in front of him and his smile falls away instantly.

"Dammit, leave me alone. I'm taken. I've told you before I'm not interested. Get a life," he growls at her before side stepping around her and heading toward me.

She looks like she's just been struck. Her jaw drops, and I try to hold back a laugh, but Kelsey fails and snickers out loud.

Denver walks right up to me and wraps his arm around my shoulder and kisses the top of my head.

"Congrats on the game." I look up at him. Something about his just-showered hair with a few water droplets still clinging to it sends tingles down to my belly.

"Thanks, it was all you. You're my good luck charm. Now, any interest in going to the football party tonight?"

"Not really." I scrunch up my nose at the thought.

"Good. Let me feed you two." He starts walking us toward the parking lot.

"Or we can go home, order pizza, and watch some TV on the couch. The game was enough peopling for me for today," I suggest.

Denver laughs. "Kelsey?"

"I'm going to meet up with Ollie. You okay to get a ride home with Denver, Avs?

"Of course, see you tomorrow. Be safe." I hug her.

"Always," she calls behind her as she runs off to her car.

"You sure you okay with me coming over?" Denver asks. I like that he is wanting to respect my limits. It makes me feel safe around him.

"Yeah, it's just pizza and TV. Don't get any bright ideas."

"Slow as you want, sweet girl." He winks as we get in his truck.

We stop by my favorite take-away pizza place on the way back and in no time, we're settled on the couch and he picks up the remote.

"What does Friday night Avery normally watch?" he asks, placing the remote on his chin like he's thinking about what to put on.

"This is usually my catch-up night, so it's normally The Bachelor or Dancing with the Stars. But I've also started watching Big Bang Theory over from the beginning, so we could watch that."

"Sheldon, Penny, and Leonard it is." He smiles and flips through my DVR.

Once we are done with the pizza, he puts the rest in the fridge for me. I pull the blanket off the back of the couch and snuggle in. He pulls me up to his side and I rest my head on his shoulder.

I am strangely calm and relaxed in his arms. We have only been out a few times since dinner at his mom's place but knowing he's my Titan makes me comfortable around him. He kisses the top of my head and I look up at him.

"You are so beautiful, Avery, but seeing you out there tonight in my jersey was something I've been dreaming of for a while now. I hope you'll come to more games and wear it."

"I'll try my best," I tell him, which earns me that crooked half smile again and stirs up flutters in my belly.

At some point, I guess I drifted off to sleep, and I wake in his arms as he lifts me up.

"Denver?" I murmur.

"Shh go back to sleep, sweet girl, I got you. Which room is yours?"

"Right side," I sigh.

He lays me down on the bed and my eyes get heavy again.

"These jeans won't be comfortable for you to sleep in, can I take them off you?"

I nod but don't open my eyes. A minute later they are slowly being pulled down my legs and then hear them land on the floor. He pulls the covers over me and kisses my forehead.

"Get some sleep, sweet girl, we have a date tomorrow."

"Mmmm, night."

Chapter 10

Avery

The last few weeks since going to Denver's football game following the date at his mom's house have been busy with studying, finals, dates, cuddles, and planning our trip to Nashville.

Denver has gone out of his way to make time for me and I've seen him every day, even if it's just him stopping by for a few minutes before he heads home or when he brings me coffee between classes. We text every night and have fallen asleep on the phone together a few times.

We haven't done anything more than kissing and a couple of light make-out sessions, but that's been enough to set my body on fire when he is near.

Today I am on the road to Nashville, with Denver driving and his mom chatting with me from the back seat where she insisted on sitting.

Football season is now over so that has freed up a lot of Denver's time, but these next two weeks will give us plenty of time together. It's four days before Christmas Eve so we have a few days to ourselves before my parents fly in.

"So, tell us about this house, Avery, I can't wait to see how you want to decorate it!" Denver's mom, Gina, asks.

"Well it was built in the 1920's and my grandparents bought it when they got married. It's four bedrooms and four baths and in a good part of town, so even though it needs a bit of work, it still appraised higher than I expected. I know I don't want to sell it. Not yet, anyway. When my grandpa died, my grandma started working on the house and said finally she could do it the way she wanted. I think she just needed a distraction from missing him."

I smile thinking of the times they would fight over wallpaper or paint colors.

"If you plan to keep it, are you going to rent it out?" Gina asks. I can see her eyes sparkle when I talk about what I'd like to do to the house.

"Yeah, I don't need the money, but I hate the thought of it sitting empty for the next almost two years. I hired the neighbor's boy next door to do the landscaping and keep an eye on the place. Since the yard is pretty big it keeps him busy and the hours are flexible since he is in high school so he can work it around his schoolwork and football. He is always sending photos of the place; he loves doing the work because I insisted on paying him what I'd pay a company. He's making more than most kids his age do."

"That so sweet, he sounds like a good kid," Gina says.

"Oh, he is. When I told him, I was coming up for Christmas break, he got his parents to help put up all my grandma's Christmas lights. She did the house up every year. He even sent me a picture of a Christmas tree in the living room they set up, saying it wasn't Christmas unless the place was decorated and there was a tree up in the front window."

Denver smiles and takes my hand as his mom talks about design and how she hopes some of the original 1920's features are still in the house. Denver smiles at me and whispers so only I can hear him.

"Our first Christmas."

I can't help but smile back. "The first of many, I hope."

"Me too, sweet girl, me too."

As we enter Nashville city limits, I give him directions on which highway to take. We drive past downtown and get some amazing views of the buildings and even Titan stadium on our right. Gina takes it all in. I love watching her eyes light up over it and I know it means a lot to Denver that she gets to see it.

As we enter the Belle Meade neighborhood, Denver's eyes go wide. He remains quiet even as we park in front of the 1920's Tudor home that was a second home to me growing up.

"This is your grandparent's house?" he finally asks.

"Yeah, it wasn't the fancy part of town when they first moved in." I shrug.

He turns to his mom who doesn't know the area as well. "This is the best part of town."

"He means the most expensive," I say with a smile. It needs some work done to it, but I still remember the day the appraisal came back at just over one million dollars. I cursed and thanked my grandparent's multiple times that night.

I watch Gina's eyes dance over the front of the house. I know she is going to love helping with it.

Just then, Eric comes running out of the house next door.

"Miss Avery! Do you like it?"

"I love it, Eric. It looks just like it did when my grandma lived here."

"I'm so glad you came back for Christmas. It isn't Christmas without this house all lit up."

My eyes water a bit. "Yeah, this is my first Christmas without her. I was going to miss the lights too. To come home and you having it all done for me means more than you know."

He blushes.

"Can I ask a favor?"

"Anything, Miss Avery!"

"When the snowfall comes and coats the yard and the house, will you send me a few pictures before the snow gets disturbed? I'd like to get a picture of the house in each season to frame inside."

"I love that idea!"

"Thanks. Oh, I have been rude, this is Denver and his mom Gina."

Eric's eyes go wide, but he recovers in record time. "Hey, good game against Alabama. We're huge MGU fans and have been rooting for you!"

"Thanks," Denver says, and I can tell the praise makes him a bit uncomfortable.

"Before I forget, Mom wants you to come over for dinner one day while you are here," Eric says.

"Would Sunday work? My parents don't get in until Monday."

"I'll let her know, we normally eat at six."

"Perfect we will be there at five to catch up. I know your mom likes to have drinks before dinner."

Eric smiles. "See you then, let me know if you need anything. I need to go tell my dad the Lightning Bolt is next door. He won't believe me!"

He runs off back to his house, making me laugh.

I turn to Denver. "How did you get the nickname the Lighting Bolt?"

Denver shakes his head. "Between my last name and someone making a joke that I run as fast as a bolt of lightning, it just stuck."

I nod and turn to look at the house that holds some of my best childhood memories. It's been months since I've been here, and this is the first Christmas without my grandma. Seeing the house done up with the lights and decorations, it almost feels like I'm going to walk in and the house will smell like her famous chocolate chip pecan cookies and she'll be there to wrap me in one of her hugs, and demand I tell her everything going on at school.

I don't realize I have tears running down my face until Denver walks up behind me and wraps his arms around my waist.

"I hate your tears, tell me what I can do to make them stop," he whispers in my ear, before turning me to face him. He uses his thumb to wipe them off my face and then kisses my temple.

"I wish I could promise there won't be any more, but this is my first Christmas since she died, and this was her favorite holiday. She loved it so much it was infectious. It is my favorite holiday because of her." I take a deep breath and paste on a smile. "You ready to see the house?"

Gina's eyes light up and she heads to the door, Denver takes my hand as we follow. I don't know how hard it will be to walk these rooms again, but I'm hoping having Denver here will make it a bit easier.

Chapter 11

Denver

I hate seeing the tears on Avery's face, but I get it and I am so happy I can be here for her and that she's letting me into this part of her life. There is no place else in the world I'd rather spend Christmas than with these two women who mean the world to me.

Avery leads us through the front door into a small foyer that opens to a beautiful living room. It's bigger than the living room, kitchen, and dining room of my mom's house.

"The fireplaces have all been inspected and are sound and working." She points toward what looks like an original brick fireplace. "They are wood burning and perfect for hot chocolate around the Christmas tree." She gets a far off look in her eyes as she looks at the tree in the window.

"The first thing to go is that creepy mirror above the fireplace. I'd like it if we can take it down tonight. As a kid, I was always scared I'd look up and some creepy little girl standing behind me or something."

I can't help but laugh as I imagine a little Avery running around the house, it sure does pull on my heartstrings.

She starts talking to my mom and I watch as my mom comes alive. She loves decorating and it was always her dream to do that for a living, but she can't afford the cut in pay to get her foot in the door.

"This room just needs a paint job and a way to organize coats in the foyer. The layout is a bit choppy, but I'd like to find a way to make it work for now," Avery says as she trails her hand along the walls. Watching her walk through the house, she has a far off look in her eyes. She has a new spark of life in her and getting to see this side of her means more to me than I can describe.

"These hardwoods are in great shape, are they original?" My mom kneels down and runs her hand over the wood floor.

"Yes, my grandma had them redone about five years ago and she took good care of them."

We walk into the kitchen and even I know this would be my mom's dream kitchen down to the water faucet over the stove to fill pots.

"I bet you can't wait to cook in here, can you, Mom?"

"Oh, this kitchen is beautiful!"

"This was my grandma's dream kitchen; she spared no expense here. She watched a lot of Food Network cooking shows and said she wanted to feel like she could host a show in her own kitchen. Feel free to use it as much as you want. My grandma said the kitchen is the heart of the home and is meant to be used. She would be mad if it wasn't used while we are here."

She leads us from the kitchen to a butler's pantry and through a teardrop shaped arch to the dining room.

"Oh, that arch is original! Please tell me you want to keep it." Mom runs her hands over the wood.

"Oh, yes, I don't want to change much, and I want to keep all the original details. It's what made this house a home. Look here at this nick in the wood..." She leans down and points to a dent in the wood a few inches off the ground. "This is where I ran into the arch while I was roller skating around the house during a blizzard one Christmas. We were stuck here for a week, so Grandma and Grandpa moved all the furniture out of the way and make a skating track for me, before they redid the floors, of course."

She stops at a half bath downstairs that hasn't been redone. The wallpaper almost looks like old newspaper clipping all over the wall but as you get closer you can tell it's all one big piece.

"This is the only bathroom that hasn't been redone and it's because my grandpa loved the wallpaper, but they couldn't find any more of it to be able to put it back up when they redid the room. I want to try and save some of this wallpaper and frame it for decor in the house before this bathroom gets torn up. Silly, but I remember my grandma trying to bribe my grandpa to let her take it down and he would always refuse. After he died, she left it as a memory of him." She smiles and runs her hand over the wallpaper by the door.

I take her hand and squeeze it. "It's not silly. I love the idea."

She leads us upstairs next. "This is the master. You can see part of the leak I was telling you about by the fireplace. The fireplace is fine, I had it checked, it's just this part of the wall that needs to be fixed. Grandma redid the bathroom here to match the kitchen. She loved the countertops so much she brought them up here too."

"It's smaller than I would've expected." My mom takes a look in the master bath.

"Yeah, when my grandparents bought it there was no master bath. They combined two rooms to make this room and the bathroom. My grandma didn't need much space to get ready, so she refused to make the bathroom too big. The master only needs paint and some decor. Gina, you should stay in this room."

"Oh no, dear. This is your room. Denver and I will take one of the others."

"But I insist."

"That's a deal breaker. This is your house, your grandparent's room, so it's your room. I won't stay there."

I watch as Avery relents and nods.

Mom walks down the hall to check out the other rooms, but I stay behind with Avery.

"Everything okay?" I ask her.

"I've never stayed in this room. Never been able to. Maybe with you two here, I can finally do it."

I pull her into a hug since I don't have the words for this moment.

"Go pick out your room." She smiles.

I find my mom in a bedroom that overlooks the backyard and she is staring out the window.

"Taking this room?"

"Oh, yes, I love it in here. The back yard is like something from one of those Christmas movies it just needs some snow."

"My grandma used to say that all the time," Avery says from the doorway.

Avery finishes her tour, showing us the basement with the laundry room and a craft room. She and Mom talk about different ideas of things they can do down here.

This house suits Avery, I can see her in every room. She has so many stories from which of the antiques creep her out and why to how several dings and dents ended up in the doorways.

"Why don't you take your bags up and get settled, then we can head out to the store get some dinner and a grocery shop. I also need to pick up boxes and tape," Avery says.

I am upstairs in the room next to the master unpacking my stuff when there is a light knock on the door frame. I look up to see Avery.

"What made you pick this one?"

I shrug. "It's next to yours."

She smiles. "This was my room growing up." I look around, it's done is yellows and greens but there is no sign of it being a girl's room.

"I had a dollhouse in the corner over there and I loved watching people drive by looking at Christmas lights this time of year from that window. I'd get myself in trouble because I'd be up past midnight just watching."

She steps in and heads to the window and looks out, lost in thought. I walk up behind her and wrap my arms around her. After a minute she turns in my arms to face me.

"Thank you for being here, it's made it a lot easier."

"There is nowhere else I'd rather be. This place has a magical quality to it, I can't explain it. I'm always here for you, Avery, always have been, even though you didn't know it."

She wraps both hands around the back of my head and pulls me in for a kiss. The moment my lips touch hers she is deepening the kiss into one filled with passion. My heart races, there is a connection between us that is above and beyond what has been there before. Forgetting where we are and who could see us, I push her up against the window trying to eliminate any space between us. The need to be closer to her is all I can think about. When the cold glass hits her back, she gasps.

"Denver," she whispers.

"Yeah, baby," I whisper against her lips as I try to catch my breath.

"Your mom..."

I groan. I know my mom could walk in at any time so with one more quick soft kiss I pull back and take a deep breath. I know in my gut that this is just the start of us. Something has shifted here. I can't put my finger on it, but I know with all certainty that I'm not letting Avery go.

CHAPTER 12

Avery

Once they are all settled in, we head out to explore Nashville for a bit.

"I have an antique dealer coming tomorrow to look at some of the stuff that I don't plan to keep. What's worth anything he will take to his shop to sell on consignment or buy outright. My dad refused to be here for that, though." I laugh and shake my head.

"Too hard for him to sell the stuff?" Gina asks.

"No, the guy is my mom's old high school boyfriend." We all laugh. "He's a good guy, came out not long after him and my mom broke up. He and his husband now run the store. They adopted a little girl who I ended up going to high school with and we became good friends. When he heard of my grandma's passing, he called and asked that I don't sell anything without him there. He never once tried to get the sale, he just wanted to make sure whoever I brought in didn't rip me off. It was never a question in my mind that I'd give him the sales. My dad still grumbles about it he can't get past that it was one of my mom's ex boyfriends."

We get back home from the store with boxes for packing up some of the rooms and food. Pulling into the drive and seeing the lights on makes it feel like home. It feels right to be here. I must have been standing and looking at the house longer than I thought, because Denver wraps an arm around me.

"Everything okay?"

"Yeah, just feels like home." I smile as we head in.

Gina insists on making dinner so she can use the kitchen and Denver helps me as we start packing things up. We pack up clothes to donate, along with lots of family photos to keep. My dad left me the keys to his truck so I can move stuff into their basement before they get home.

Before I know it, it's after 10 p.m. and we all say good night and head to bed. As I climb into bed, I check out my grandparents' room and try to imagine it as my own. Could I live here? I'd love nothing more than to have a family and raise my kids here. I have to find a way to make it my home and not like I'm tiptoeing around after the ghosts of Grandma and Grandpa.

I'm lying in bed, coming to terms with the fact that I plan to live here and make a life here, when my phone goes off.

Titan: You up?
Me: Yeah lots of memories, it's hard to sleep.
Titan: Lots of noises I'm not used to.
Me: Yeah. I still have you listed as Titan in my phone.
Titan: Leave it. I like it.
Me: Okay.

There is nothing back from Denver, so I keep thinking about moving in here after graduation when my door opens and Denver slips in. He lies down on the bed next to me but over the covers.

"What is your favorite memory in this house?"

I stare at the ceiling for a moment, the past filling my head. "Pretty much every Christmas. Grandma loved decorating and it always started before Thanksgiving by sorting decorations and buying news ones. I have photos of all the decorations. She would make sure every room was done up, even the bathrooms. The house was always one on the Nashville Lights Tour. A few years when I was in high school, she even won some awards."

He smiles and reaches out to take my hand. "Worst memory?"

I don't even have to think. "Both Grandma and Grandpa's wakes were held here."

He turns on his side to face me and I do the same. There is just enough light from the open curtains and the nightlight in the bathroom to make out his face.

"My mom loves this house. She lights up when she talks about decorating it and I haven't seen her like that in a long time. So, thank you."

"Has she ever thought about becoming an interior designer?"

"She never could go back to school for it, and now to get her foot in the door, she'd have to take a pay cut. She can't afford that and to still put me through school. If I can get signed into the NFL, it will give her the chance to do it. I'll encourage her to as well."

I shake my head. "It's a talent you can't be taught, either you have it, or you don't. Listening to your mom's ideas, she has talent. Do you think she'd like to help me with this place? It could be the first in her portfolio."

He smiles. "She would love that, Avery. You should talk to her."

I nod. "Good, because I want someone I can trust working on this place."

We lie there for a few minutes before I speak again. "I've been thinking tonight, and when I get out of school I want to live here. I can't bear to sell it. It's hard being here and making changes, but the thought of selling it is more than I can bear. It just feels so big for one person."

He reaches up and tucks some hair behind my ear and traces his thumb across my cheek. "Don't sell it. Make it your own. Your grandparents would love for you to raise a family in their home."

I think about that. I know my grandma would love having her great-grandbabies here and raising the next generation in this house is exactly what they wanted. "I will."

I smile and his eyes lock with mine.

"Avery..." he whispers before his hand goes behind my neck and pulls me into him for a light and sweet kiss that gears up to a passion-filled tango. His tongue meets mine and it's like he is making love to my mouth as his hand grips my hair and pulls me closer.

My breasts rub against his chest causing him to groan and pull away just a bit.

"Every time I kiss you it's better than I remember from that first night," he whispers against my lips.

"I was just thinking the same thing." I snuggle up with my head on his shoulder and he wraps his arms around me, pulling me close. I'm so comfortable and I feel so safe that I don't think twice about drifting off in his arms.

Chapter 13

Denver

I don't sleep much that night with Avery in my arms. I want to soak up every minute of it, memorize the feel of her pressed up tight along my side, her body heat soaking into me, the sounds she makes when she sleeps and the scent of her shampoo.

I drift off at one point and wake to watch the sun filtering in the bedroom windows. Not too much later, Mom peeks her head in to find Avery still in my arms.

"We stayed up talking and she fell asleep like this. I didn't have the heart to wake her," I whisper.

Mom smiles at me. After the first night that I brought Avery home, she hasn't stopped talking about her. She loved her and thought she was the sweetest girl. It helps that my mom knew what Avery meant to me and how we met.

"I'll start some coffee and breakfast, you two come down when you're ready." She quietly closes the door behind her.

I gently rub Avery's back. "Beautiful, it's time to get up, the antique guy will be here in two hours."

She groans and rolls on to her back, stretching her arms above her head, emphasizing how thin her T-shirt is, and the fact that she isn't wearing a bra underneath it.

I can see she is as turned on by being so close to me. Her nipples are stiff peaks and tenting her shirt which makes the hard on I've been fighting all morning spring to life. When the hem of her shirt lifts just enough to see a sliver of her belly, come starts leaking from my cock and causes me to groan. I try to shift around and adjust myself, but it does nothing with her so close.

She rolls back to her side and looks at me. "I haven't slept that good in a long time. Thank you for staying with me."

Her eyes travel down my body and I know the moment she sees how hard I am because she gets the sexiest blush on her cheeks.

"Sorry," she mumbles.

I lean over and tilt her chin to look up at me. "Sorry for what?"

She doesn't say anything, but her eyes slide back down to my cock, making me smile.

"Yes, sweet girl, that is what you do to me and I'm not sorry. I'm also not going to push for anything. I didn't wake you when you fell asleep because you felt so good in my arms."

She smiles and leans in to kiss me, pressing her chest to mine. Her hard nipples brush across my skin and my mind goes blank at how good it feels.

In the next minute, she wraps one leg over my hip and pushes her core against my hard length, grinding against me. Her hands snake down to the top of my sweatpants and I grab it back up.

"Sweet girl, not right now."

She bites her bottom lip and nods, but has an unsure look on her face how does this girl not know I want to spend the rest of my life inside of her.

I groan and roll to my back, pulling her on top to straddle my hips and get a better angle. She places her hand on my chest for leverage and slowly grinds back and forth on my cock, every thrust making her moan.

I cup her breast over her T-shirt and rub my thumb across the hard peak of her nipple. This time her moan is louder, so I pull her down and kiss her jaw and along her neck to her collarbone, before sucking her nipple into my mouth over her shirt. I give it a good suck and a slight nip as she starts wiggling her hips against me again.

I give the other nipple the same attention before grabbing her hips and helping her find a steady rhythm while grinding on my cock. She runs her hands under my shirt and up my chest, and all I can do is close my eyes and enjoy the sensation of her skin on mine. Her hands feel amazing on my chest. I can't help the shivers that take over my body as she moves at an agonizing slow pace.

When I can't take it anymore, I flip her over onto her back. I stretch her arms above her head and grind into her.

"Denver," she gasps.

"Yeah, baby?"

"Don't stop."

"I couldn't if I tried."

I kiss down her neck and grind into her harder causing her back to arch, and I barely cover her mouth with mine before she lets out a moan with her climax. Her shorts are thin enough I can feel her pussy flutter with her orgasm and it's enough to have me coming in my pants.

I rest my head in her neck and work on catching my breath as she wraps her arms around my neck and plays with my hair which causes small trembles down my body.

"You okay?" she whispers.

I smile into her neck "Yeah, that is all you. God, I haven't come in my pants since high school."

A blush creeps down her neck. "I'm sorry."

I kiss her neck and trail kisses up to her jaw. "No, that was the sexiest moment of my life, don't apologize." I can see it in her eyes that she doubts me.

"I'm sure you've had better." She looks away from me.

What is running through her head? I've never come so hard in my life and she thinks I've had better?

"Look at me," I whisper. "Why would you say that?

She shrugs, but when I don't let her break eye contact, she takes a deep breath. "Kyle always said the reason I never got off was because I was a bad lay."

The amount of anger I have for Kyle right now is something I've never felt in my life. If we were back at school, I'd hunt him down and give him a proper ass beating. How dare he make this amazing and sexy woman doubt herself. How dare he tear her down like that when he is the one with problems. My heart bleeds that she has thought this about herself all these years. I can't wait to prove to her what a sexy goddess she is.

"Fuck, sweet girl, he is such an idiot. I'm not like him. I haven't been with anyone since my high school girlfriend and she was my first. I kissed you that night and knew I wanted you. *You*. But by the time I found you again you were dating him. I waited. I know this will make me sound like an asshole, but I prayed it wouldn't last. I knew what I felt from that one kiss and I haven't kissed anyone since that night."

"Why did you walk away that night? He told me your girlfriend was calling."

I jerk back. "No, it was my mom. Who's he?"

She sighs. "Kyle."

"So much got messed up. If Mom had waited and called ten minutes later. If I'd gone with my gut that summer and moved her like I wanted to, we could have avoided all this. I would have gotten your name and number and it would have been us dating all this time. Kyle wouldn't have been tearing you down for his own inadequacies. Baby, I wouldn't have been able to stop myself from coming just now, even if I tried. It was so powerful because it was you. It was us. This is still the sexiest moment of my life, better than anything I ever imagined."

With tears in her eyes, she pulls me down for the sweetest kiss that breaks my heart and heals it all over again. After a moment I pull back.

"Avery," I whisper against her lips. "Say you are mine. Sweet girl. I need you to be mine." She smiles against my lips, but she doesn't answer. I pull back and when she opens her eyes, her forehead wrinkles and she rubs her lips together like she does when she is thinking before she answers. I know she has been hurt before, and I know with everything that I am I will wait as long as she needs.

"If you say no, just know I'm not going anywhere. I am not stopping. I've been waiting this long for you and I will keep waiting. I'm not giving up."

"Don't break me, Denver," she whispers.

"Never, baby. Be mine." I brush my lips against hers again.

"Yes, as long as you're mine, too."

"I've been yours from the moment of our first kiss."

With that, she smiles and in that moment under me, her blond hair spread out on her pillow, and that gorgeous smile on her face, she looks more beautiful than I have ever seen her.

"Let's head downstairs, I smell breakfast," she says.

I sit up and watch her bounce off to the bathroom and I can't wipe the smile off my face. Avery Hayes is finally mine.

Chapter 14

Avery

I don't know what guys talk about when they say they need a cold shower. I took one and it hasn't helped. The second I'm downstairs and my eyes land on Denver my body remembers what we did in bed and I'm on fire again.

This is going to be a long day.

They don't see me yet and I stop when his mom starts talking.

"Good morning, I guess? You can't seem to wipe that smile off your face," Gina says.

"The best morning. She agreed to be mine."

"I know you like her and have for a while, so I'm happy for you. I like her too."

That makes me smile. I make some noise like I am just getting downstairs and enter the kitchen. "Good morning."

"Hey, sweetie. There are pancakes and coffee."

Denver hands me a cup of perfectly made coffee. "Thank you."

He kisses my temple. "Go sit down, I'll make you a plate."

I smile as I head to the dining room. To have him take care of me like this warms my heart and makes me feel loved.

Whoa, Avery. Let's not break out the L word, we just officially got together this morning. But Titan's texts fly to my mind all those weeks ago, him telling me he had been waiting for me. He wouldn't wait over two years if it wasn't serious, right?

Before I can finish that train of thought, Denver sets a plate in front of me and sits down. He runs his hand over my thigh under the table. "Eat up, sweet girl."

The heat of his hand on my leg burns through my leggings. I swear he knows exactly what it's doing to me because he smiles and brushes between my legs just slightly before pulling his hand away to eat breakfast.

Once his mom sits down, we start talking about the plans for the day and about Carl, my mom's ex-boyfriend, and his husband Simon.

Just as we are finishing up, the doorbell rings. Gina grabs our plates and takes them to the kitchen. I stand to answer the door but first reach over and brush my hand across Denver's crotch. "Game on," I whisper in his ear, then walk away.

It takes him a full minute before he can stand to join me in the hallway, and it makes me smile. Carl and Simon both greet me with a full hug.

"Look at how grown up you are! I remember when you ran around the school, always with the biggest smile, and now you're an adult." Simon shakes his head.

"I'm sorry about your grandma, she was the sweetest woman. One of the first people I came out to." Carl offers me a sad smile.

"I didn't know that. But I do know she would have been supportive and by your side the whole way."

He nods. "That she was."

I invite them inside but when Carl looks a little hesitant, I can't help but laugh.

"My parents aren't here; they won't get back in town until Monday."

He relaxes and smiles. "How are your parents?"

"They're doing good. Enjoying traveling since I've been away at school. They did an Alaskan cruise this summer, before coming home to spend summer vacation with me." I trail off because our happy summer vacation ended when my grandma died.

A strong hand wraps around my waist and I know Denver is there, offering me support. I wrap my arm around his and turn to him and smile.

"This is..." I pause for a second and decide to go for it. He is spending his Christmas break here with me and helping me, I can give him this. "...my boyfriend, Denver."

The smile that takes over Denver's face is worth it. He rests his forehead to mine for a minute then rubs his nose against mine before pulling back.

"This is his mom, Gina. Guys, this is Carl and Simon." Everyone exchanges hellos before Carl starts looking around.

"Well, where do you want to start?" Carl asks, and I can tell he is excited. He loved some of the items my grandma collected.

"Let's start with the creepy mirror. Oh, I forgot to ask, will you be able to give me an idea of value for some of the things I plan to keep as well?"

"Oh, of course! We are all yours for the day." Simon glances around the house with an eager eye.

I show him the mirror Denver helped me take down not long after we got here. They love the old, bubbled glass. By lunchtime they have loaded up twenty-seven items including the mirror, the bedroom set from the 4th bedroom, three display cabinets, one of which falls into the creepy furniture category. Also, two antique chairs, several end tables, paintings, and some lamps.

"Please tell me you will stay for lunch," Gina says as they load up the last lamp.

"We'd love to!" Carl smiles and looks around at some of things they're not taking with them, while Simon helps Gina make sandwiches for lunch. Carl stops in front of the cabinet holding my grandpa's fishing lure collection.

"What plans do you have for these?"

"I hadn't thought about it. Mom and dad already took everything they wanted. I remember grandpa always collecting them, but he never used them. Why do you ask?"

He laughs and Denver comes to look at the collection beside me.

"These are very old. This one here," he points to the one on the top row, "Came up for sale at an auction a few years back and sold for just over two thousand dollars."

I don't think I heard him correctly. That's more than that stupid creepy hutch was is worth!

Denver coughs then whispers, "Holy shit." Before looking at me then rushing to my side and giving me support, because I'm sure the shock is written all over my face.

"What?" I ask Carl, just to clarify what he said. I can't take my eyes off the fishing lures I watched my grandpa collect my whole life. There must be over a hundred of them in this cabinet.

"Well, from what I know, the ones on this top shelf would be over a thousand each. A few I would need to look up. It seems he had them organized. These two middle shelves hold lures that are around five hundred price range. It looks like the ones on the bottom might have been for fun, they aren't worth much, about a hundred each. I do see ones mixed on each shelf that he must have collected for himself that hold no value, like this Mardi Gras colored one."

"No, those are the ones I bought him." My eyes tear up and Denver's hands grip my hip. I lean into him. "He mixed my cheap gifts in with his expensive lure collection. I didn't know."

"Avery, I bet those lures you gave him meant more to him than any of the others," Denver whispers in my ear

All I can do is nod. I know he's right. Carl studies them a bit longer.

"I'd do my research on each one, but at a rough guess, I'd say you have a one hundred k collection here."

I'm lightheaded and barely notice Denver guiding me to sit down on the couch. He kneels in front of me.

He takes my face in both his hands. "Sweet girl, look at me." When my eyes meet his, he whispers, "Breathe. I got you." I nod and rest my forehead to his. A move that is quickly becoming comforting.

"I didn't know," I whisper.

"I know. I got you, I'm right here."

After a minute, I look up at Carl and he offers me a smile.

"I need to think about it, but my grandma collected a few things I should have you take a look at after lunch."

Over lunch Carl shares stories of my grandparents and my mom. They even talk about my dad and that he doesn't hide the fact he doesn't like that Mom dated him. He has us laughing by the end of lunch. Gina offers to clean up while we keep going.

"Well, next would be my grandma's cookie jar collections, I guess." I lead them to the butler's pantry. "She would switch out the one on the counter every few months based on the holiday or her mood. My dad took a few and there are a few I'd like to keep, but I planned to get rid of the rest."

"Well, let's pull them out and set them on the counter. I can take a look," Carl says, but I can see a spark in his eye.

We do just that and as I set the last one on the counter, he looks at me. "Do you know the story around this one?"

He is holding up the creepiest of the jars. It's the head of a black lady with a creepy smile on her face. It's meant to be a representation the Mrs. Butterworth lady, but I think the artist was way off base.

"She said she found it at a flea market in Virginia. She stopped putting it on the counter when I burst into tears once saying its eyes followed me and it scared me." I smile. "I haven't seen it again until now."

Carl looks at it and smiles. "This is a Gilner Mammy Cookie jar. On most of them, the lady is dressed in yellow, but this one is white which makes it very rare. Last one I saw at auction went for $1300, but there hasn't been one for sale in over ten years."

Instantly Denver is behind me with his hands on my hips again offering me support, letting me know without words that he's there for me.

"But that isn't the most expensive one of the bunch," Simon adds.

"No, of course not," I murmur.

"This Donald Duck one is extremely rare. It was made for the high-up Disney executives one year. We know of only four others and the last one sold for over ten thousand dollars." Simon smiles at me.

I lean back against Denver and close my eyes. I can't process that these cookie jars from some of my favorite childhood memories are worth so much.

I watch Carl pick up one that looks and pick up another one "This crystal one is worth about two and a half."

"Two and a half dollars?"

"No. Two and a half thousand."

"Oh my God, I remember that one being on the counter so many times. Just sitting there for me as a kid to take cookies from. I never thought anything of it and she never acted like any of these were worth any money." I shake my head.

"Those are the highest valued ones. You have a few worth a grand, some a bit less. If I had to price this collection as it sits? You ready?"

I take a deep breath and feel Denver's thumb rubbing circles on my hip, so I nod.

"I'd have to say the collection is worth about two hundred and fifty thousand all in."

I squeeze my eyes closed again. "Dammit, Grandma."

"I was planning to sell most of these anyway. I just had no clue they were worth so much."

"Which ones are you looking to keep? I can give you a ballpark price on them for your records."

I point out a few and he nods. And fills out a form for me for my records. I place the ones I plan to keep back in the cabinet and then decide to call my dad. I walk to my grandpa's study getting ready to sit on the couch when Denver sits first then pulls me on to his lap.

"Thank you for being here. I'm just in shock."

"I bet. Call your dad, I'm not going anywhere."

My dad's phone rings a bit before he picks up. "Hey, cupcake. Going well with Simon?"

Normally the fact that my dad won't say Carl's name would make me smile, but not right now.

"Did you know the fishing lures grandpa collected were antiques?"

"I knew they were old, why?"

"Well, I just got an estimated value of one hundred thousand for the set."

"Holy Shit." The fact that my dad just cussed with me on the phone says everything I need to know. He never cusses in front of me or any lady, if he can help it.

"Yeah, I haven't touched them. I don't know what to do with them. But it gets better. Grandma's cookies jars? The set as it stands right now is worth two hundred and fifty thousand"

I listen to my dad curse more than I had ever heard him my whole life.

"I had already decided which ones I was going to keep and had planned to get rid of the rest. I guess I will just put them up for consignment. You got the ones you wanted, right?"

"Yes, cupcake, we got everything we wanted from the house already."

"Anything else I should have them look at before they leave?"

"Maybe the books in grandpa's study? They are all leather-bound, but I have no idea which ones are new or old. I never paid much attention to them."

"Okay." I look around the study at the bookshelves filled with leather-bound books.

"You okay there?"

"Yeah I brought someone with me who I want you to meet. He and his mom are helping with the house. I hope it's okay they have Christmas with us."

"*His* mom?"

"Yes, Dad, I brought my boyfriend home." I watch Denver's eyes light up.

"How long have you two been dating?"

"Well the dating part is new, but we have known each other since freshman year and been friends for a while. He was planning to come help me as friends before the boyfriend thing happened."

"Okay, I can't wait to meet him. Here's your mom."

"New boyfriend?!" Mom screeches, making me laugh. "I want the details and I need a picture."

"Mom." I laugh.

"Okay, Okay. What are your plans for the weekend?"

"Well once we finish here, I'm officially going to go into shock. Then tomorrow night we have dinner next door."

"Oh, I love the Burns family. Tell them hello from us."

"I will. Can you text me that wine she likes and the cigars he likes? I want to pick some up for them."

"I'll text them when I get the picture of you and your new beau."

"Okay, Mom." We both laugh and say goodbye.

Denver nuzzles my neck. "I like that you called me your boyfriend to your parents."

"Yeah?"

"Yeah." He kisses a trail up my neck.

"Well, my mom is withholding information from me until I send her a picture of you. So how do you feel about taking our first official couple selfie?"

"Is this a for-your-mom-only selfie or one I can post to my social media and tell everyone you are mine."

"You can share it."

"Good, stand up."

He walks up behind me, pulls me back into his chest, and leans his head next to mine. I put my phone up and take a picture of us both smiling.

"Take one with my phone?" He hands me his phone.

We are standing the same way, except this time when I go to snap a picture he leans in and kisses my neck.

He looks at the pictures. "Perfect, send me the one you took, and I'll send you this one," I say as I text the first one to my mom and she replies quickly with the information I asked her for and a few heart emojis. My aunt taught her about emojis last year and she has been overusing them ever since.

There is a knock on the door frame and look I up to see Carl.

"Hey. Dad said to have you take a look at these books too, some he says are old, but neither of us paid much attention to them."

We spend a few hours in the study, and he pulls out several books all worth a few hundred dollars each that I send with him to consign. By the time they leave, I am emotionally drained but so happy I have Denver by my side. I can't imagine trying to do this alone.

It doesn't escape me that he was here and knew exactly what I needed. Kyle wouldn't have even given a second thought about ditching me. Then I remind myself to stop comparing Kyle and Denver. I already know Denver is a much better man, he's proven it time again, and now he's mine.

Chapter 15

Denver

I save the photo of Avery and me as my background on my phone and I plan to share it everywhere later. I want to scream from the rooftops that she's finally mine.

Once Carl and Simon leave, I can tell she's overwhelmed.

"Why don't we get out of the house?" I ask her.

"Yeah, I need to do some shopping. I want to pick up a few things for the Burns' before we go to dinner tomorrow and we need wine. Lots of it. Let's have dinner while we are out too, my treat."

"Avery, you will not be paying while we are dating."

"This isn't a date and I want to thank you guys for today and celebrate my grandparents being crazy collectors."

I shake my head and laugh.

We head to the mall and she finds the wine and cigars easily and as we pass the sports shop her eyes light up.

"I know what to get Eric! Come on." She ducks into the shop and I hesitate for a moment before following her.

"Denver Bolter? No way!" The middle-aged man comes around the counter to greet me.

I just smile.

"I'm Jerry, I own the shop. I can't believe you're in my shop."

"Well, my girl here is looking for something, but hasn't told me what." I smile over at Avery.

"I want one of your jerseys," Avery says, and walks to the MGU section.

"I can get you one back at school."

"I need it tomorrow, for Eric, so I want to buy one here."

"Oh, we have them right here..." Jerry shows her.

"Perfect. Eric can open the jersey then you can sign it in front of him while his parents get photos. I saw his eyes light up when he met you."

"You can have the jersey if you sign one for me," Jerry says.

"I appreciate it, but we'll pay for the jersey to stay on the good side of the NCAA. I'm happy to sign one for you though."

"Of course, sorry, I wasn't thinking," Jerry says and shakes his head.

I smile and sign the jersey for him as he rings Avery's purchase up and then I take a picture with him before we head out.

"I think Eric is going to be over the moon to spend dinner with you. He's a good kid."

I smile. "He reminds me of myself at that age. I saw him out back practicing earlier. He could have a good football career in front of him, if he keeps his head on straight."

My mom meets us back at the car holding a few bags that she loads into the trunk.

"Where do you want to go for dinner?" I ask Avery.

"What are you two in the mood for?"

"I'd love something local, not a chain," Mom says.

"I know just the place." Avery smiles and gives me directions.

"Loveless Cafe?" I ask her.

"You can't get any more Nashville then Loveless."

We walk in and find out there is an hour wait, until the manager recognizes me.

"Are you *the* Lighting Bolt?"

"That's what they call me." I smile but I'm a little uncomfortable with all the attention I've been getting today.

"Oh, man, you are a legend around here! My dad is going to be so mad he went home early! Can you wait here a minute?"

I nod and look over at Avery who shrugs and smiles. I take in all the signed pictures that cover the walls that range from Elvis Presley and Johnny Cash to Kenny Chesney.

"My dad has this picture hanging in his office. If you would sign it, I can get you seated now, we just had a table clear."

I'm not used to all this fanfare back at school, but then again, Mountain Gap is a small town. I glance over at Avery and she is looking back at me, her eyes shining. Not a single bit of resentment over the attention. Mom has such pride on her face it makes my heart burst. I realize then that I do all this for these two and if moments like this make them this happy, I hope they never stop.

I sign the photo and take a picture with the guy before he takes us to a table at the back of the dining room.

"I don't know if I will ever get used to what a big deal you are." Avery shakes her head once we sit down.

"I'm not used to it. It's not like this back at school."

"Well, I'm so proud of you, baby. I knew you'd grow up and do amazing things," Mom says.

"What's good here?" I ask, hoping to change the subject.

"Everything." Avery laughs.

I get a BBQ sampler platter, Avery gets fried pork chops, and Mom gets the fried chicken. We all share food and talk. There are so many smiles around the table. Avery loosens up and seeing her and my mom together, is better than I imagined it ever would be. We share a few slices of pecan pie before we head out.

"That food was so good, I can't remember the last time I was this stuffed!" Mom jokes.

"Oh yeah, I need to grab something real quick, I'll meet you guys out at the car," Avery says.

"We can go with you," I offer.

"No, it's okay, I'll just be a minute." She smiles and winks at me.

A few minutes later, I get a text.

Avery: Pop the trunk.

She included a wink face emoji and one holding his finger to his mouth in a shushing emoji.

I follow her request and a minute later she is back and putting something in the trunk.

***

Avery

As soon as his mom started raving about the food here, I knew the perfect gift for her. I went back and got a large gift basket with a cookbook, biscuit mix, a few other mixes, and their jams. They even gift-wrapped it for me.

Now I just need a gift for Denver. I'm thinking about it as I make my way back to the car and place the basket in the trunk. A man walks by with a Tennessee Titan shirt on, and it hits me. The perfect gift.

When we get home, I sneak away and call my dad and tell him my idea. He says he can do it but needs to make a few calls first.

Once we get settled, we watch a few Christmas movies before his mom heads up to bed. I get a text from my dad telling me it's a go and he was able to line everything up. I smile at how quickly he pulled it off.

"Why don't we go get ready for bed and then snuggle up in my room to watch a movie?" I ask.

He nods and we head upstairs. We are cuddled in my bed watching TV when I look up at him. "Thank you for today, by the way."

He pulls me closer. "Nowhere else I'd rather be."

I lean up and kiss him. I mean for it to be a short, sweet kiss, but something ignites in me the minute my lips touch his. I pull his head down to mine, deepening the kiss, and I can't seem to get close enough. I swing my leg over his hips and straddle him just to get closer.

We spend the rest of the movie making out like teenagers. I can feel how hard he is under me and I am so turned on, I know we both need relief.

"God, I want you so bad," I say to him between kisses as I grind down on him.

"I want you too, sweet girl, but our first time is not going to be with my mom down the hall. But I will always take care of you."

Before I know what, he is doing, he has me flipped over onto my back. He runs his hands up my thighs and over my hips. One of his hands finds my core. I have on thin cotton shorts that I love to sleep in, and I can feel the heat of him through them.

"I can feel how soaked you are. Can I take off your shorts?"

All I can do is nod because there is nothing that I want more. He slides the shorts slowly down my legs and then runs his rough hands across my skin. He pushes my legs wide and positions himself between my thighs. He runs his nose over my panties before moving them to the side.

"So beautiful," he murmurs to himself as he rubs his thumb over my clit causing my hips to jerk and my breathing to hitch in my throat. "And so responsive."

Then his tongue is on me and I lose the ability to think, all I can do is feel. The warmth of his tongue circling my clit, the electric pulse waves radiating off of me and pulling at me to fall over the edge. His five o'clock shadow rubs against my thighs, and the vibrations of his moans pulse through me.

As he sucks on my clit, I grab his hair and hold him in place because I don't think I could stand it if he stopped, but in the next moment he moans, and it pushes me over the edge. I have enough thought to grab a pillow to cover my face as I come harder than I ever have before in my life.

"Wow." I try to catch my breath. He places a kiss on the inside of each of my thighs before tugging my underwear back in place and kissing his way up to my lips.

"That's how I felt watching you come undone like that. I've never seen anything so beautiful." He kisses my neck and then rolls to the side so his weight isn't on me.

I look over at him and sit up. His eyes track me as I make my way to him.

"My turn." I smile.

"No, sweet girl, this was about you."

"And it's still about me, because I want this."

"Avery, I love going down on you and I don't expect anything in return."

I grab the hem of his pants and start to pull them down. He doesn't try to stop me.

"All the more reason I want to do this. Plus, why wouldn't I love to go down on you and watch you come apart for me?"

Denver squeezes his eyes closed and tosses his head back on the pillow. He lifts his hips and helps me get his pants and his boxer briefs out of the way.

Now I'm getting my first look at his cock and boy is it impressive. Long, hard, and thick with come dripping from the tip. I can't let that go to waste. I lean down and lick the come off and he groans.

I look up at him and when his eyes meet mine, I slowly take him into my mouth as I watch his breathing pick up. He never takes his eyes away from mine.

I work him in and out of my mouth, taking more each time until he hits the back of my throat. I use my hand on the base. When his hand runs through my hair it makes me moan and his hips jerk.

"I'm so close, Avery. God, your mouth feels like heaven."

I suck harder but this time I bring my other hand cup his balls before giving them a light tug and it's enough that he starts to come in long hot spurts down my throat. He pulls a pillow over his face seconds before he lets out a long groan. I swallow down every last drop and when he removes the pillow from his face, he is breathing hard. I give the head of his cock a kiss before climbing back up him.

When my eyes find his there is almost a look of wonder in them.

"Come here, baby." He pulls me up to him and tucks me into his side. "I've never felt anything like that, I can't even explain it."

"That's how you made me feel." I snuggle into him with my head on his shoulder. "Will you stay with me tonight."

"I don't think I could get out of bed if I wanted to, but I definitely don't want to." He kisses the top of my head and pulls the blanket over and sleep pulls me under.

Chapter 16

Denver

My heart is racing, and I can't catch my breath. It's the same feeling I have when I wake up after having a sexy dream of Avery, except this time the pleasure is still building.

When I open my eyes the sight in front of me steals what little breath I have left. Avery has her mouth around my cock again and before I can even stop myself, I'm coming down her throat.

"Holy fuck, that is one hell of a way to be woken up."

She gives me a smile and I pull her up to me for a kiss.

"That was the best way to be woken up. But it's your turn now."

I flip her over and take my spot at what is now my favorite place in the world, between her thighs. She is wet and already close to orgasm.

"Did having your mouth around my cock do this to do you, baby?" I lick her desire off her lips.

"Yes," she gasps.

"I don't think you know what that does to me." I thrust two fingers into her and watch her hips buck. "Knowing how turned on you are by my cock in your mouth. I don't have the words for it." I suck on her clit, running my tongue over it faster and faster until she falls apart for me.

I kiss my way up her body, paying attention to her breasts over the tank top she wore to bed. I've gone down on my girl twice, but I've yet to see these gorgeous tits that have been tempting me for years.

I slowly inch up her tank top, kissing up her stomach as I do. I pause a second before her breasts come bouncing out of the fabric. They are perfect, full, and round, with dark pink nipples.

I look up at her and she is watching me with her lips slightly parted. I grab one in each hand, they are a bit more than a handful. I massage them memorizing the feel of them in my hands.

"I love these," I tell her, but I don't take my eyes off my hands. I lean down and suck one into my mouth while I pinch the other nipple. Then I turn and do the same to the other. I don't want to ever let them go but the need to have my arms around Avery wins out, so I tug her tank top back down.

I lie down beside her pull her into my arms, kissing her shoulder, neck, and the top of her head.

"I don't want to get out of bed." Avery sighs and wiggles against me. There isn't an inch of space between us and I love it.

"Well, it's not even 9 a.m. I think we can get away with lying here a bit longer," I tell her.

"Tell me about your favorite Christmas memory."

I can't help but smile. "One year my mom worked on this big project with her boss, she was the secretary then, but she was working some long nights to help out. I remember going into the office a few times over Thanksgiving break. They won the contract and her boss, who is a nice guy, gave my mom a raise and a weekend away at his cabin in Gatlinburg. So, we went up the day after Christmas for five days. Just being in the mountains with a bit of snow and all the lights around town was magical. We walked downtown and got hot chocolate, some homemade donuts, and fudge."

"It sounds amazing."

"It was, my mom loved that cabin, but we could never have afforded it. That's why I bust my ass in football. If I can get into the NFL, I can give her things like that and take care of her like she did me."

Avery places a hand on my cheek. "You are amazing. You take care of her more than you realize, Denver, and she looks at you like you hung the moon. If the NFL is what you want, then I know you will get there and do it, because you are good.

Really good. But make sure it's what you want too."

"I have everything I want right here, right now. My mom is happy and safe, and I have you in my arms. I've wanted this for so long, Avery, and now that you're here with me, I feel like I can do anything."

"You *can* do anything." She looks up and gives me a shy smile. "I have a confession."

"Uh oh, good or bad?" I tighten my hold on her.

"Good for you."

"Well, color me intrigued."

She laughs. "I wasn't ever one of those go-to-every-football-game girlfriends, but even when I was dating Kyle and I was at the game I watched you more than I did him. I was there when you got the ball at the Arizona game and ran it forty yards. I was cheering so loud for you I lost my voice the next day."

This girl. Does she even know what a simple confession like that does to me?

"I was always hoping you were watching at the games. I lied to myself often telling myself you were, I would push harder for you, to make you proud."

"God, Denver, I am so proud of you. I always have been, you are an amazing, strong man and I'm sorry I didn't see that the first night."

I kiss her forehead. "We are right where we are meant to be, but I smell coffee, so I also think we need to get downstairs."

We spend the morning packing up the den and pulling everything out of it since it's the room that needs the most work. I swear she timed it so every time I looked up, she was bending over a box with her ass facing my way, teasing me.

After lunch, I find Avery and my mom in what was her grandpa's study.

"Any idea what you want to do in here?"

"I think I want to keep it an office. I don't need as many bookcases, but I still need to go through the books. I think I'd like to keep a bookcase full of his books in here. I know he would write in the margins of some, so those I want to keep for sure, but I want to brighten it up."

"Well..." Mom starts, looking excited. "We can do that by removing the thick curtain and replacing it with something a bit lighter, and some lighter furniture. Maybe a pale gray paint on the floor and large rug under the desk and chair to save the wood floor, and then another rug over by the bookcases to define a seating area. If you want to make it more feminine, we could add a chandelier and some faux crystal accessories."

"I love that idea. You will help me a this, right?"

"Of course! Do you want to go through some books in here, we still have a few hours before we have to head next door?"

"Yeah, can you guys start going through books and set aside any that have my grandpa writing in the margins or are autographed?"

"On it," I say and kiss her temple.

***

We are getting ready to head next door for dinner and Avery and my mom have decided to get ready together. I'm downstairs in the living room staring out the front window watching the cars go by.

Every day I'm in this house it feels more and more like home, more and more like Avery. I'm starting to be able to see a future with her, a life with her here. Our kids playing in the front yard in the snow during the winter or in the sprinklers in the summer, maybe with a dog running around with them.

I can see summer nights on the back porch swing while the kids catch lightning bugs and watching the stars come out. Barbeques, birthday parties, and sleepovers. I want it all with her. I want the NFL so badly, it would be a dream to be drafted by the Tennessee Titans so I could stay here in Nashville, buy my mom a place nearby, and then fix this house up for Avery any way she likes.

I want to spoil her and give her the life I know she is starting to see in this house. I see it cross her face when she starts thinking about what she wants to do in each room. I love watching it dance in her eyes as she slowly gets more and more excited about making this place her home.

I turn when they come down the stairs and I have a hard time catching my breath. She is in dark jeans that look like they were painted on, a loose red sweater, and short ankle boots. There are curls in her hair, and she looks so beautiful. I hope I get to see her come down those stairs and knock my breath out many more times in our life.

"You ladies look amazing. May I have the honor of escorting you next door?" I hold out an elbow each to Avery and Mom.

As we walk over to the Burns' house, I can't help but think how perfect this all is.

Chapter 17

Avery

I have always loved having dinner over with Greg and Laura. They are so warm and bubbly, but right now, watching them talk football with Denver, is one of my favorite moments. He is in his element talking about his games and other players.

He next to me on the couch with my hand in his and while he is talking to Greg and Eric, his thumb is running over the back of my hand. Eric hangs on Denver's every word about college football. I figure now is as good a time as any to give him his gift.

"So, a little birdie told me your favorite wine, Laura." I smile and pull her wine from the bag I brought with me. "And your favorite cigars, Greg."

"Oh, Avery dear, thank you so much! This is perfect, I've only one bottle left!"

Laura says.

I smile. "Now, the rest of this bag is for Eric."

"Thank you, Miss Avery." He pulls out Denver's Jersey, and his face lights up. "Thank you!"

"There is something else in there." I can't help but smile when he pulls out a Sharpie marker with a confused look on his face. When he looks at me, I look at Denver and when Eric realizes Denver is going to sign his jersey for him, he gets so excited he starts bouncing up and down.

"I can't believe I'm going to have a signed jersey from the Lightning Bolt, oh my God! Mom, Dad, get pictures!"

They spend a few minutes with Denver signing the jersey and taking pictures and Gina watches the whole thing with a huge smile on her face. I scoot down the couch to sit next to her.

"Do you ever get used to this?" I ask.

She shakes her head. "I'm sure you see it more than me, being at school with him. When he comes home, he's just Denver. He does dishes, takes out the trash, helps with yard work. He doesn't act any different and I don't treat him any different."

"There isn't as much fanfare at school as you might think. It's a small town there and being here in Nashville is the first time I've seen people fawn over him. Well, other than the Jersey Chasers." I roll my eyes.

"Ahh yes, he's complained about them before. Said he wants someone who wants to be with him for him. Not for a ride to the top or the money. Then in the next breath, he's always be telling me how you weren't like that and that he needed to find a girl like you. The longer you were with Kyle I think the more he started to think it wasn't going to happen with you and him."

I shake my head. "I didn't know. I felt the connection but to think he wanted me, that he was waiting for me all this time. There's no way I could have known."

"I know, and he is loyal to the team, so he would never have let on."

When Denver comes to sit next to me again his mom winks.

"What are you ladies whispering about over here? Care to share with the class?" he jokes.

"You and how proud of you we are." I kiss his cheek and watch a light pink stain his cheeks which makes me smile even more.

Over dinner, Greg, and Laura share stories about me growing up. From the time Eric and I built a whole family of snowmen in both front yard after the big snowstorm several years ago, to how excited I was when Eric was born and how I got to hold a baby.

I smile and shrug. "I was an only child and always wanted a brother or sister. Eric's the closest thing I got."

Eric's face lights up. "It always felt like I had a sister with you around. I never cared that I was an only child. It sucked when you went away to school."

"Well, the plan is I will be back when I graduate next year but then you will be the one going off to school. Any plans on where you want to go yet?"

"I plan to apply to both University of Tennessee and Mountain Gap. I'd love to stay close to home. But my adviser said I need to apply to ten places total and not plan on getting a football scholarship offer."

"I was told that too," Denver says. "I applied at UT, Mountain Gap, Ohio State, Alabama, Georgia, a few in Florida, Mississippi, well basically all the southern universities plus Ohio, because they have a great football team. But I knew I wanted Mountain Gap so when I got the offer, I took it and didn't wait to see what else came in."

"Do you regret jumping on it so fast?" Greg asks.

"Not for a second. It was where I wanted to be, close to my mom, close to Nashville and Knoxville. It was my first choice, so I didn't see the point in waiting to see what else came in. I knew freshman year I'd made the right choice."

He looks over at me and my heart races. That choice led him to me. It was set in stone from the time I was a kid and knew I would go to Mountain Gap. I never thought about attending any other school. It's where my parents met, it's where my grandparents met. That thought makes me laugh.

"What is so funny, beautiful?"

"I never thought I'd go anywhere else. My parents met at MGU and my grandparents too." I shrug and watch Denver's eyes soften.

He leans over to whisper in my ear. "And now we've met. The tradition continues." Butterflies take over my stomach. He surely can't mean what I think he does. We just started dating he can't be that sure about me. He's a football player and has his NFL career ahead of him, god only knows where that will take him. It's crazy to be thinking like that. The rest of the dinner the conversation flows and reminds me that this is my favorite time of the year.

***

I am on the way to the airport to pick up Mom and Dad. Gina insisted on staying behind and make sure dinner is ready, and as much as I wanted Denver to come with me, he said I should have some family time and he wanted to help his mom in the kitchen, so I didn't argue.

I park and make my way to where everyone else is waiting on their loved ones to come through the gate. The Nashville airport has become a second home to me since I've been at school. Anytime I want to come home, my parents fly in and I meet them here. They have no problems taking a taxi but there is something about meeting family at the gate that I love.

Mom sees me before I see her because I hear her call out, "Avery!" causing heads to turn. She runs up and wraps me in one of her huge mom hugs. Then holds me at arms' length for a full mom inspection. This has become routine since I went away to school.

"Your hair is longer," she says.

"Yes, I like being able to pull it up when I'm studying."

"You've gained weight."

I roll my eyes. "Blame Kelsey bribing me with cupcakes, but now I'm dating a football player, I'll lose it trying to keep up with him."

"You will do no such thing. I'll have a talk with that boy, you need to put on a few more pounds. You've always been too skinny!"

"Speaking of... where is this boy?" Dad looks around.

"Back at the house, his mom insisted on cooking dinner for you and he stayed to help her saying he wanted us to have some time together."

"Which means he knows we're going to be talking about him." Mom drapes her arm over my shoulder and leads us to the door.

"Any bags?" I ask.

"Nope. We sent some stuff on to your house, it should be there in a few days. That way we could just have the carry-on luggage and switch things out while we are home. Just put the box on the kitchen counter when it comes, dear," Mom says.

I laugh as we head out to the car and as a true southern man, my dad insists on driving, so I end up in the back seat of my own car on the way home.

"So, tell me about this boy, how did you meet? How did you start dating? What exactly happened with Kyle?" Mom rapidly fires questions at me.

"Ugh, Kyle cheated on me many times, apparently. I know things were different after Grandma died, but he pulled away instead of helping me through it. It was over when he didn't come to the funeral, but I had too much going on to deal with it."

"I never liked Kyle," Dad grumbles.

"I know, Dad, and that was always in the back of my mind. Grandma told me it's important for the right guy to get along with those closest to me. That's you guys."

"Oh, so what about Denver? He's a cutie!" My mom can barely contain her excitement.

I grin. "We met freshman year at the freshman welcome party. The football team was doing dares to the new freshman and his was to kiss me. He came over and we talked for a bit then he fessed up to the dare, so I kissed him and there was something there. I thought so at the time, anyway. But he got a phone call and left. I met Kyle and we know the rest."

"So how did you reconnect?" Mom urges me on.

I smile. "He was on the team with Kyle, so we were on friendly terms," I tell them about how he got my number and was texting me as Titan and helped me ditch Kyle and get out of a bad blind date. It doesn't escape me that my dad took the long way back to my house as he listens to every word. I finish my story just as we pull on to my street.

"He sounds like a good guy, but I'll reserve my judgment until I meet him." My dad gives me a pointed look in the mirror.

"I wouldn't expect anything less, Dad."

"You guys put the lights up?" Mom asks.

"Actually, Eric and his dad did when they found out I was coming home. They even got us a tree and put lights and tinsel on it. They left wood for the fireplaces too."

When we pull up the driveway, Denver is out the door to greet us. He opens my mom's door first and she greets him with a big hug as my dad opens my door for me.

"Come on, let's get inside. I hope it's okay I started a fire in the fireplace, you said they were checked and working, the temperature is supposed to drop and there is just something about a fire on Christmas Eve," Denver says.

"It's perfect!" I smile back at him.

"Mom made a roast, her rolls, and dessert. She loves cooking in that kitchen." He takes my hand as we head into the house.

I laugh as the warm air greets me and we take off our coats and shoes.

"It almost feels like she is still here," my dad says softly right next to me. "With the fire going, the tree up and the smell of dinner from the kitchen."

My eyes tear up. "It does, doesn't it?"

"No more tears please, sweet girl I don't think I can take them today." Denver runs his thumbs under my eyes, making my mom smile.

"Sorry, this is Denver. Denver, this is my mom and dad."

"Nice to meet you." Mom smiles at him and doesn't hide the fact that she is checking him out.

"She been crying a lot?" My dad asks with concern on his face.

"Yeah as we go through things, some memories. Though I won't lie, I love hearing her talk about those memories and growing up here."

"Oh, hi! I'm Gina." Denver's mom says as she comes out of the kitchen. "Dinner will be ready in about fifteen minutes."

She hugs my mom and shakes my dad's hand, and her and Mom disappear into the kitchen, and I know that look in my dad's eye.

"That my cue to go help in the kitchen," I say. "Be nice to him, Dad, he isn't Kyle."

"We'll see about that."

I turn to Denver. "I want to say call me if you need help, but really you're on your own." I kiss his cheek and head into the kitchen.

"Where's the wine?" I ask.

My mom hands me a glass. "Figured you'd want this with them in there together."

"Thanks."

Gina smiles. "That boy would walk through fire for you, Avery, he will hold his own just fine against your dad."

"You haven't met my dad. Though I'm sure Denver has had plenty of meet the dad experiences." I look back toward the living room but can't hear anything. I know he's only had one other girlfriend but I'm sure there have been other dates.

"Actually, this is only his second meet-the-dad that I know of. He had a steady girlfriend in high school, but when he got the football scholarship, she became a stage five clinger and was talking about changing school for them to be together. It was like she became a Jersey Chaser overnight. He broke up with her and refused to date until he got to college, then he met you."

"He didn't date anyone all this time?" Mom asks, shocked.

"Nope, he's always been talking about Avery. Did she tell you their first date he brought her home to meet me?"

"He promised me fried chicken to get me out of a bad blind date, then said you had won awards for it, how could I say no?"

We chat a bit more about school and Kelsey as we work on setting the table and getting things ready, and I can't help but stop and take a look around. Both our families melding together so well. The house, for the first time since grandma passed, feels warm and is full of love, laughter, and life, just like grandma always wanted, just like I always told her I wanted.

"Thank you, Grandma." I send up a whisper of thanks before the boys join us for one of the best Christmas Eve dinners I can remember in a long time.

Chapter 18

Denver

I wake up and it hits me that it's Christmas morning. I look at the angel in my arms and I know I have everything I could ever want right here. It hits me hard and without an ounce of doubt that she is it for me. She is mine.

It's been slowly washing over me since we have been here in Nashville. I know it's too early, we just became official on this trip and it's been just over a month since she's known I'm Titan, but I knew she was special the first time my lips touched hers.

All the time she was dating Kyle, I watched her, got to know her, and fell in love with her from a distance. I don't think I wanted to admit it to myself but that's what it is. Love.

I love Avery Hayes.

I look at her asleep in my arms and if I didn't think she'd shove me out on my ass, I'd ask her to marry me today. She has been burned by Kyle and I know it's hard for her to trust in general, much less a football player. Then there is the NFL draft, it leaves so much in the air, but I know I want her by my side, I need her by my side.

I'll fight for her, for us, and prove that her taking a chance on me was the best choice she ever made.

I rub her back, as much as I want to let her sleep, I want to give her gift alone.

"Hey, sweet girl, it's Christmas."

"Mmmm, merry Christmas, Denver," she mumbles as she opens her eyes.

I reach over to the nightstand where I put her gift last night.

"Merry Christmas." I hand it to her.

"Denver..." I watch her open it and find the necklace with my football number on it. "Oh, Denver, I love it."

"I know when I hit the NFL the number will change, but this is who I am now. Who I was when we met and when I finally became yours. It's our number, Avery, number 18."

"It's also how old we were when we met." Avery smiles and my breath catches. She's right. 18 really is our number.

"And..." She trails off and reaches for her phone. Then shows me a text message. It takes me a minute to realize it's the first one I ever sent her, sent on September 18th.

"Do you believe in fate?"

"I'm starting to."

We get up and get ready and head to her parents'. Her mom insisted on making homemade cinnamon rolls for breakfast while we open gifts and spend the day together.

The moment we walk into her parents' house, the smell of cinnamon hits me and it doesn't escape me how much this place feels like home from the moment I'm in the door.

We are sitting in the living room and I'm watching Avery pass out her gifts. She got my mom a gift basket from Loveless café, and my mom hasn't put the cookbook down since. She rented a cabin in FL for her parents' next trip, so they have their own space instead of staying with her mom's sister like they do every year.

Then she turns to me. "Your gift is the last one to be opened so you are going to have to wait." She shrugs.

"I got you to agree to be my girlfriend, that's the best gift you could ever give me."

Both Moms let out a chorus of, 'Awws' and I just shake my head.

"Me next!" My mom jumps up. She got Avery's parents' a travel journal and they gush about how they love the idea and wish they had thought about it sooner. When Avery opens her gift and it's just a photo frame, I'm confused why she has tears in her eyes.

"How did you do this?" she asks my mom.

"Last night while you were sleeping."

She turns the frame around and in it is a large piece of the wallpaper from the downstairs bathroom that she had said she wanted to frame to place in the house.

"I mentioned this to you just a few days ago, how did you make it happen?"

"I have my ways." Mom smiles.

"That damn wallpaper." Avery's dad shakes his head but smiles too. "You are going to redo that bathroom, right?"

"Yeah, I wanted to keep some wallpaper though. This is perfect, thank you."

"Here you go, baby." Mom hands me a wrapped box. I open it and my eyes go wide. Inside is a special edition box set of my favorite mystery book series.

"It gets better, open the cover," Mom says.

I open the cover to find them personalized and signed.

"Mom?"

"He did a book signing in Nashville a few months back. I talked to my boss about it, and he had some stuff to do in Nashville, so he took me into the city dropped me off and picked me back up. I even still got paid for the day."

"I think he likes you as more than his assistant, Mom." I smile she waves her hands at me.

"Don't start, Denver." Mom gives me a stern glare.

"Our turn." Avery's mom pops up and passes out a small box to my mom whose eyes go wide when she opens it.

"What is it?" I ask her.

"Season tickets to your games next year." My eyes dart to her parents. I know those tickets aren't cheap. As it is, I only get four tickets all year to give away and I give them to my mom because she uses every one of them. But having season tickets and knowing she will be at every home game is an emotion I can't explain.

"Thank you," Mom whispers, overwhelmed with their kindness.

"Well, Avery mentioned how you only get so many tickets each season and I know as a parent who lived so close, I'd want to be at every game. This way you can be. Those seats are near his team's benches too."

Mom hugs both of them and then me too.

"Here, sweetie, we didn't have time to add Denver's to your gift but his goes with yours, so open it together." Avery's mom hands her a box.

Inside the small box is a plane ticket and before we can ask, her mom starts talking. "Good for anywhere in the USA any time over the next year. There will be one for Denver too. We figure you two can maybe go somewhere spring break and get away from school for a bit. You need the full college experience and I know you haven't done a spring break yet. Plus having a bulked-up football player to watch over you can't be a bad thing."

Avery looks at me. "Mom is always pushing me to make sure to do all the college experiences, parties, beer pongs, spring break, football games... all of it."

"You only get this chance once, make the most of it." Mom adds.

Now I'm up. I hand a gift to her parents.

"I wasn't sure what to get you, but I thought you might enjoy this."

Their eyes light up as they start flipping through the photo album, I put together of photos I was able to find of Avery at school.

"Where did you get these photos?" her mom asks in awe as Avery leans over to take a look.

"Most of them are from football events. I asked a few of her friends for some, Kelsey has an abnormally large collection of photos of you, by the way." I look over at Avery.

"Oh, I know. It's a thing with us, I have a ton of her too."

I hand my mom her gift bag. It's a day at a Nashville spa while we are still here. She never gets pampered and I want to make sure she will be. Avery helped me plan this one because I don't know a thing about day spas.

"Thank you, baby!"

"You're going to go while we are here in Nashville, non-negotiable." I give her my stern face and she smiles and nods.

"And he already gave me my gift..." Avery shows off the necklace I got her.

What no one knows is that I found that necklace over a year ago and knew it was perfect for her and bought it then, not knowing the significance of the number 18, other than it was my number. Not knowing if I'd ever have the chance to give it to her. I love seeing it on her now. It looks better than I ever imagined it would.

"Okay, now for your gift." Avery hands me an envelope but it doesn't escape me the large smiles on her parents' faces and how she is almost bouncing out of her seat.

I carefully open the envelope and take out the paper inside, taking in Avery's excitement one more time before looking at the paper in front of me. It takes me a minute to register what I'm looking at.

"Avery?"

"My dad pulled a few strings and got the three of us a private tour at the Titans Stadium. He has a friend who works there who will be showing us around. I know the Titans are where you want to end up and I know you wanted to show the stadium to your mom." She shrugs.

"Come here, beautiful," I whisper.

I don't care that our parents are in the room and three sets of eyes are on us, this girl just gave me the perfect gift. I pull her in to me with my hand behind her neck and kiss her hard.

"Thank you," I say against her lips, and place one more soft kiss there before pulling away.

I face her dad. "Thank you for this."

"It was all Avery. I just made a phone call." He nods.

The rest of the day is spent baking cookies, eating, and talking. Her parents get to know us and in return share stories of young Avery, making her blush a few times.

Chapter 19

Avery

I dropped mom and dad off at the airport yesterday and they told me they really like Denver and hope I bring him home again soon.

Today we have been loading boxes in my dad's truck and taking them to the room in my parents' basement for storage, this way when or if I rent out the house it's all out of there. My plan is once I move in myself and I'll bring the boxes back and go through them properly then.

Denver is driving us to my parents' place on our last run of the day and Gina insisted on staying back to make dinner and try out my grandma's bread maker. She really does love that kitchen.

Denver has been holding my hand the whole drive and talking about the stadium tour because my dad texted me the time and instructions for tomorrow.

We get the boxes unloaded as he is setting the last one down, I just take him in as his muscles flex and strain under his shirt. He catches me watching and stalks over to me and before I know it, he throws me over his shoulder and is carrying me back up the basement steps with me laughing the whole way.

He sets me down in the kitchen. "Stop staring at me like you want to rip my clothes off, sweet girl."

"Maybe it's because I do."

He growls but I just smile and look toward the ceiling.

"You know I've always had a fantasy of sneaking a boy up to my room but never got the chance."

"Yeah?"

"Yep. Do you know anyone who would be willing to fulfill my fantasy?"

"You better be messing with me, beautiful, because if any other guys end up in your room, they're likely to lose their life."

I hold out my hand with a smile and he takes it, following behind me on my way up the stairs.

He walks into my room and I stop at the door to take him in. This hulk of a football player standing in my childhood room full of my stuffed animals, awards, and a few boy band posters on the barely-there purple wall paint. Mom and dad haven't changed the room one bit.

He glances around before looking back at me and walking over and placing his hand on my waist.

"You never snuck a boy up here?"

"Not once."

"You coming in or staying there?"

I smile and step in and close the door, then pull him down for a kiss. His hands trail up my sides under my shirt and brushes his thumb along the bottom of my bra.

"Ever make out with a boy in this house?" he murmurs into my neck.

"No, I didn't spend much time here with boys."

His hands trail up a bit higher and I speed the process up by reaching down and removing my shirt. His breath hitches as I reach around to remove my bra as well.

"God, you're beautiful."

I know I have to be blushing. I drop my gaze, but his finger is right there under my chin tilting my head up.

"That blush is sexy, Avery, don't hide it from me."

I take a deep breath and nod. He reaches behind himself and pulls his shirt over his head. Seeing all that tan skin and muscles makes my head spin. This sexy man that all the girls at school are lusting over is mine.

I slide my pants off then walk over to my queen-size bed and lay down in the middle.

"You going to join me?" I ask. He eyes me hungrily and nods, removing his pants until he is in just his black boxer briefs as he climbs into bed with me. He runs a finger over my lips, down my neck, between my breast to my belly button.

Then he continues down to the top of my black lace underwear and traces over the fabric.

"Mmm, nice and wet for me."

I arch my hips trying to get more friction and he smiles. He pulls the fabric aside and strokes my clit at the same time he takes one of my nipples into his mouth. The dual sensation washes over me and my hand flies to his hair and I moan out his name.

"That's right, baby, no one here to hear us." His mouth moves to my other breast and he thrusts two fingers into me while using his thumb on my clit.

"God, you're so tight."

I gasp when he takes my breast again, sucking harder this time as he curls his fingers inside me, hitting that perfect spot that makes me buck my hips and explode a second later screaming his name.

"Fuck, I love how loud you are, such a turn on."

He pulls his fingers out, causing me to whimper at the loss. He brings them to his mouth, sucking off my juices and letting out a moan.

"I think I'm addicted to your taste." He moves to go for more, but I stop him.

"I want you, Denver," I whisper.

"You are about to get me."

"I want you inside of me."

He stops moving and closes his eyes.

"You sure about this, Avery?"

"Yes, this is my fantasy after all. I'm sure you felt how wet it made me seeing my sexy, muscular, football player boyfriend standing in my room. Can't you feel how much I want this."

"Avery..."

"Denver, I want this so much," I say and my heart races.

He studies my face and takes a deep breath. When he stands up, I think he's about to leave but he reaches for his wallet, pulls out a condom and sets it on the nightstand.

He kicks off his boxers. I run my eyes over him as he strokes his cock a few times before taking a deep breath and climbing back into bed.

He kneels over me and hooks his finger in the side of my panties and slowly slides them down my legs and tosses them on to the floor. This is the first time we have been completely naked in front of each other and it's not awkward, it's a turn on seeing Denver hard and ready for me.

"I don't think I've ever seen anything so sexy, baby. You laid out naked and wet for me, I can see how wet you are from here."

He reaches for the condom and rolls it on without taking his eyes off me. He runs his hands up my legs then pushes them wide and settles between them. He takes my hands in his as he rests on his elbows and holds my hands above my head.

The head of his cock is at my entrance, but he pauses.

"Denver," I whisper his name and he smiles softly at me.

"Just give me a minute, baby, I want to remember everything about this moment. How you look under me, the desire in your eyes, the feel of your skin on mine. There is no turning back after this, Avery.

It would break me if you walked away now."

God, this man has the sweetest heart under his buff exterior. Knowing only I get that side of him soothes my fears in a way I didn't think possible.

"I'm not going anywhere. I'm right where I'm meant to be. I feel it."

"Eyes on me, baby." His voice is hoarse with passion. I can't remember a time when a guy wanted me so much, it's empowering and has me dripping and ready for him.

My eyes meet his and he slowly slides into me never breaking eye contact and lets out a long, loud groan.

"Oh, god, you feel so damn good." He pulls out and slides back in. "So tight." He buries his head in my neck as he gives one more thrust and fills me. He pauses there and, in that moment, skin to skin, feeling so full, something shifts within me. I'm tethered to him in a way I can't explain. Like I'm not me without him.

It's never felt like this, so right. He starts slowly thrusting, pulling halfway out and then sliding back in. He lifts his head and his eyes meet mine and while no words are spoken so much is said.

As he picks up speed my nerves start to tingle through my body and pressure builds in my core. His lips take mine and he stills for a moment as he kisses me. He lets go of one of my hands and slides his around my lower back and raises my hips to change his angle, making me gasp.

"I'm not going to last much longer; you feel too good."

"I'm close, too," I gasp.

He makes one little shift and hits a spot inside I didn't know existed. I instantly come so hard that I dig my nails into his back and hold on tight because I feel like I might fly away. His body starts shaking, his hand gripping mine tighter as he moans my name in my ear until he stills and his climax washes over him. When I open my eyes, he wraps his arms around me and turns us to lie on our sides not immediately pull out of me.

He is breathing as heavily as I am. I lean in to kiss him again.

"Wow," I whisper.

"Yeah."

"I didn't know..." I trail off, realizing it's not cool to talk about sex with other guys while in bed with your boyfriend.

"Didn't know what, sweet girl?"

I sigh. "I didn't know it could be like that."

A huge grin covers his face. "I should say I'm sorry but I'm not, this is us and I will make sure it always stays like this."

I smile and kiss him slow and sweet.

"Where's the bathroom?"

"Down the hall, the door on the left."

I watch him walk away and then slide under the covers not wanting to move just yet. He walks in and sets something in a bag on the floor next to the bed.

"Don't think you want your parents finding a condom in the trash."

I cringe and he laughs. Then his eyes heat and he peels back the covers to lie beside me. He slowly trails his fingers over my shoulder, across both breasts, down to my stomach, my hip, and back up.

"I can't wait to learn every part of your body, baby. I've been dreaming of this moment a lot longer than I should have been."

I take my turn and run a finger down his chest and stomach to his hips stopping just above his cock, which causes him to shiver, then I trace back up and pull him in for another kiss.

"We should get back, Mom is making dinner," he whispers against my lips.

I could stay here in our warm happy bubble all night, but I know he is right, so I nod, and we get ready to head out.

Chapter 20

Denver

Today is the private tour of the Tennessee stadium. I'm so excited to show this to my mom and to be experiencing it with Avery.

We meet Avery's dad's friend at 10 a.m. and he shows us some of the offices and then he takes us to what he jokes is the underbelly—The training rooms and locker room.

While in the locker room he talks to my mom about things like the ice bath and how they treat injured players. I walk up behind Avery and wrap my arms around her.

"One day I will play here," I whisper into her ear and turn her to face one of the lockers. "One day my lockers will be in here. You will meet me at the stadium, and I will fuck you against my locker so that before every game I have the memory of being inside you, because that will be the first thing I do when I get home every night."

She gasps, making me smile, and I nip her ear before pulling away.

We walk out and take in the view from the field. We can't walk on to the grass, but we can snap a few photos from the sidelines with the field behind us.

Next, we tour a press box and then he gives us a rare peek into the owner's suite. The view is right on the fifty-yard line and you can see the whole stadium, the word 'Titans' painted on to the seats, and the Nashville skyline behind.

One day I hope my girl will be watching me play from one of these suites.

On the way home, my mom and Avery talk about the spa day they are doing tomorrow. I plan to do a few landscaping things around the house for her to keep busy. It's a great way to end our time here in Nashville.

***

The first day back and I'm called into coach's office. That's never good.

"Coach?" I peek my head around his door and see Kyle sitting in front of coach's desk.

"Bolt! In and close the door."

I do as he asks and sit in the chair next to Kyle.

"I'm going to get straight to the point. Kyle here says you are messing around with his girl."

I dig the heels of my palms into my eyes to stop myself from going off.

"Avery is not his girl. Avery is the girl he's been cheating on all year. The one he grabbed and put a mark on at the party and got benched for. She is also the one he stole from me freshman year. I wasn't in here bitching about it because Avery can make her own choices."

"I didn't steal her!"

"I had to deal with shit with my mom, and you told her I was off talking with my girlfriend then made a move on her. She told me that's how you two started talking!"

"ENOUGH!" Coach roars. "You are *not* letting a piece of pussy interfere with this team, Bolt!"

I slam my fist down on the desk. "Don't you *dare* talk about her like that. You may be my coach, but you will not disrespect Avery like that. She's not a side piece, she is my soul mate, the girl I plan to marry. She has been it for me since I started here, but I've had to watch this sorry excuse drag her through the mud, yet I said nothing and never once let it affect the team. She is *mine* now. My everything and the one thing that will cause me to walk away from this team without looking back because there is no walking away from her."

Kyle opens his mouth to speak but coach holds up his finger silencing him. I know I just put my ass on the line for next season because no one talks to coach that way.

"Were you messing around with her while she was still *officially* with Kyle?"

"No."

Coach nods. "End of discussion. Kyle you may leave. If this comes up again, you'll be benched. Bolt, stay seated."

Kyle walks out giving me a smirk, thinking I'm in trouble. But he doesn't realize there is nothing coach can dish out that I won't take. I don't regret sticking up for Avery, not even for a minute.

After Kyle closes the door, coach sits back in his chair and stares me down. I meet and hold his gaze and neither of us says a word for a minute.

"I don't think I've ever had a player talk to me like that before."

"I won't apologize."

Coach stares me down a bit more like he's trying to make me uncomfortable, but it doesn't work. Finally, he sighs.

"I didn't know what Avery meant to you. You haven't talked about her before, so I assumed. I apologize for what I said, but if you tell anyone that I will deny it."

I smirk.

"So how did she end up with Kyle?"

"My mom called seconds after our first kiss was over. Remember when I had to go home and move her because she was having problems at that apartment?"

Coach sits back in his chair "Yeah I do."

"I tried to find her before I left that night and couldn't. By the time I got back, she was dating Kyle. I only just found out from her that Kyle swooped in the second I walked away, saying it was my girlfriend on the phone. I kept telling myself that if she was happy, I'd let it be. I've watched her from a distance, and she was happy until she came back to school this year after her grandma died. Kyle was sleeping around and coach you know I didn't let any of it affect me out on the field this year, not once."

"No can't say it did."

"It won't next season either. The night she and Kyle broke up I was there. I walked her and her roommate home because it was dark, we talked a few times after and texted, but we didn't have our first date for months. We didn't become official until over Christmas break when I went to go help with her grandma's house."

"My statement stands this better not affect the team."

"My statement stands as well, it won't on my end, but I will always pick Avery. If you put me in that spot, I'll choose her every time, no second thoughts."

"Her before the team?"

"Coach I don't ever want to let the guys down, but they are only my team for one more year. This girl is going to be my wife for the rest of my life."

"You sure about that?"

"Yes. I will go at her pace and I know, thanks to Kyle, she has some trust issues, made worse that I'm a football player too, but I'm not going anywhere and yeah soon as she is ready, I'm ready to take that step. I had a moment with her over break where it hit me hard."

"Well I'm not going light on you in front of the guys, but I will be respectful of her from here on out. Don't you ever talk to me like that again. We understood?"

"Yes, coach."

"Get out of here."

I get up and head into the locker room where Kyle gives me a smirk before walking out. Derick is by my side instantly.

"Hey, Kyle said you were getting nailed by coach."

"Everything is fine, Kyle's just trying to start trouble. I was told not to let Avery interfere with the team. I told him I haven't all this time and it's not starting on my end now. We talked, it's all good."

"Okay, you need to tell me what happened over the break we haven't had a chance to talk yet, man."

"Avery is finally mine." I can't help the huge grin that crosses my face.

"Finally!" He is the only other person who knows the whole story of what happened and how I felt about Avery. He's who I'd go to vent or drink with and there was never any judgment.

"Drinks on me later this week, I want to hear how it finally went down.""

"Deal. I need to go see my girl."

He pats me on the back before he heads out of the locker room. I finally get to say things like that. It's small and maybe stupid to others, but I have been waiting all this time to be one of the guys who leaves after practice or a game and says it's time to go see my girl.

Chapter 21

Avery

It's the first day of classes since Christmas break and I miss having a class with Denver, but at least this semester Kelsey and I are sharing an elective reading class. Not really needed for her nursing degree, and it's suggested but not needed for my writing degree, but we just wanted a class together.

The class is fun, we will be reading some classics this semester and we are talking and chatting about the books on the way home from class, so much so we don't notice Kyle on our front porch steps.

"Avery..."

My eyes snap to his.

"What do you want, Kyle?" My voice is cold. I don't like to be ambushed at my house.

"Are you and Denver together?"

"What?" Is he really asking me that question? It's none of his business.

"The guys in the locker room are talking."

"Why do you care who I date?"

"He's my teammate!"

"You cheated on her!" Kelsey yells.

"Kelsey, go inside, I got this," I say, my tone as even as possible.

"I'll be watching from the window." She throws a pointed glare at Kyle then heads inside.

"You have no say over who I do or don't date," I seethe.

"No, but he should have known better, you don't date your teammate's ex!"

"Fuck you, Kyle. I'll sleep with the whole team if I want. You sure slept with enough of the school, tit for tat, right?"

His eyes go stormy as he looks behind me, the air shifts, and I know who I'm going to see before I even turn around.

"What's he doing here?" He puts himself between Kyle and me.

"He found out that we're together and is trying to tell me who I'm allowed to be with."

"You can be with anyone you want, but my teammates aren't supposed to close in on my ex."

"So, you leave coach's office and come right here to cause more problems? Plus, we just had this talk."

"I didn't steal her from you," Kyle spits.

"Actually, Kyle, you kind of did. You lied saying he was stepping away to take a call from his girlfriend, so I dismissed him and focused on you. Now, what do you mean he just left coach's office?"

"He got me called into coach's office, trying to get coach to step in on our relationship. Jokes on him. I have coach's blessing. He found out all this has been going on since freshman year and I've not once made a problem for the team. Yet here we are not even a month in, and this is the second issue today from Kyle." Denver doesn't take his eyes off Kyle.

"You or coach have no say on who does or does not date me! You cheated on me with half of the campus." I'm about at the end of my rope and I'm not sure how I've kept my tone level this long.

I place my hand on Denver's arm because I can tell even the thought of me with anyone has him on edge.

"You chose to cheat on me, Kyle. So, you gave up the right to be pissed about anyone I date."

"Well, I wouldn't have had to sleep with someone else if you hadn't been so distant."

There is the straw that broke the camel's back.

"My grandmother had just died! I was working on dealing with her house and her will and I was in freaking mourning, Kyle. You didn't lift a single finger to help and didn't even go with me to her funeral!"

I go to lunge at Kyle, intent on ripping his balls off but Denver's hand goes around my waist calming me. Kyle's fists clench and unclench like he is trying to hold himself back.

"But more than that..." I remove Denver's hand, and lean into Kyle's ear and whisper. "If you don't leave Denver and me alone, your little drug and steroid habit will be released to your coach, the NCAA, and the press, along with the pictures I have of you shooting up."

When I step away his face is pale white.

"I didn't care what you did then, and I certainly don't care what you do now. I'm not one to go and spread it, but so help me, Kyle, if you don't leave us alone, I will spread your dirty laundry, not just in front of the school but for the NFL to find too. This goes on and off the field. Any whisper of you giving Denver trouble and it'll be game over."

The rage is still in his eyes, but he looks between us all, then drops his head and walks off defeated.

Denver is still tense and all I can do is turn to unlock my door when he speaks.

"I'm going to go," he says, but he's looking past me, not at me.

"What? Why don't you come in? I have dinner going in the crockpot."

"No, I'm good."

I sigh. "He ambushed me, Denver. I did nothing wrong and I don't like being made to feel like I did." With that, I head into the house and close the door behind me.

"What dirt do you have on Kyle?" Kelsey asks before I even make it to the wine.

"Something I won't share. I won't do that to him because it'll fuck up his career."

"Most girls would have spread it far and wide the first chance they got, especially as he cheated on you."

"I'm not most girls. Now I'm taking a bath." I grab the bottle of wine, a plate of food, and some cookies and head to the bathroom to lock myself in.

I let the hot water soothe the tension in my muscles as I try not to think of Denver walking off. I did nothing wrong and I will stand by that. The water starts to cool off, so I refill the tub with hot water and I'm just settling back when my phone goes off.

Titan: I'm not mad at you.

I am not having this talk via text message. I set my phone down and refill my wine glass. Halfway into that glass, my phone goes off again.

Titan: I just needed to cool off.

That's nice. Still not having this conversation via text. I must be drunk because tossing my phone in the toilet sounds pretty good right now.

I finish that glass and it goes off again.

Titan: Are you mad at me?

I roll my eyes. What gave it away.

Titan: Talk to me please.
Me: Yes, I'm mad. I come home from class to be ambushed by my ex-boyfriend who I haven't talked to in months, and instead of making sure I'm okay, my current boyfriend walks off. Thanks, but no thanks.

Titan: Jesus, Avery, I was so mad I didn't want to take it out on you. I went for a walk. Can I come over and talk, please?
Me: No.

I then decide to make him suffer by placing my legs on either side of the tub and making sure the bubbles cover the surface and snap a picture. It must be the wine I'm not normally this petty.

I send it.

Me: This is what you are missing out on because I wasn't important enough to check on.

Titan: God, baby, that's not it. I was so mad I wasn't thinking straight, and I didn't want to take it out on you. I went for a walk and ended up at the gym. I went several rounds with the punching bag.

My phone rings and seeing Titan is calling I send it to voice mail.

Titan: Please, baby, pick up.

My phone rings again. Silenced again.

Me: The phone ringing is kind of ruining the mood in here.

I drain the water again and refill, this time with more bubbles. I'm sure my hands and feet are beyond wrinkled but messing with him is turning me on, or maybe it's the wine. So, I slide my hand down my stomach until I reach my clit and start rubbing.

Titan: Please don't tell me you are fingering yourself in that tub.
Me: Okay, I won't tell you.

The doorbell rings but I close my eyes and ignore it. I know Kelsey will get it. Ignore the muffled voices and think of Denver's muscled body lying on my bed just the other night.

Next thing I know there is pounding on the bathroom door.

"Avery, baby." Denver's voice is hoarse.

"Mmm, kind of wishing the door isn't locked, I could use a real-life image."

"Fuck, you're killing me." He tries the door again.

"Kelsey might have a key."

"I gave her money to go to the movies and leave us alone." His footsteps soften before the sound of drawers opening and closing fill the air. He comes back and the doorknob jiggles again before it opens this time.

I look over at Denver and smile. "Live and in person, let me see those abs."

He hesitates only a minute before he rips his shirt off and falls to his knees by the tub.

"I'm so sorry, Avery, I wasn't thinking. Well, I was. All I was thinking is how much I wanted to smash Kyle's face in and how quickly it would end any chance I had at the NFL. I saw you there and I didn't want to take it out on you, so I went for a walk and ended up at the gym."

I glance at his abs and bite my lip.

"Fuck, are you still touching yourself?"

I nod and watch his Adam's apple bob. He runs his hand over my leg that is on the side of the tub and traces it all the way down under the water to where my hand is.

When his hand meets mine, his breath hitches and his eyes snap to mine. He pushes my hand out of the way and replaces it with his.

"Lie back and let me take care of you," he whispers.

I lean my head on the back of the tub and close my eyes as his thumb works my clit as he thrusts two fingers into me. I groan and roll my head to the side to look at him. His eyes are on me and they are intense as he picks up the pace. I moan, rolling my head back. He increases his thrusts and my hips jerk as he curls his fingers enough to send me over the edge. I'm drunk enough that I don't care, and I come, screaming out his name. He doesn't stop even as I start to come down from my orgasm. Another is building right behind it and it takes me quickly over the edge again before I have time to catch my breath.

This time he pulls out and grabs a washcloth and my soap and washes every part of me without a word. Then he drains the tub and grabs a towel, helping me up. He dries every part of me like I'm the most precious thing in the world, then wraps me in the towel, picks me up, and carries me to my room, laying me on the bed.

He covers me up and kisses my forehead. "I really am sorry, Avery, call me when you get up in the morning." he whispers.

"No," I say, and he stops in his tracks.

"Avery..."

"Why would I call you when you will be right here in bed with me." I pat the bed beside me, but he hesitates.

"Get your ass in bed, Denver." I give him my stern voice, and I close my eyes and snuggle into the pillow.

"Okay but let me go clean up the bathroom and make sure the door is locked."

I nod and bask in the warmth from the wine. He climbs into bed with me. His warm skin against my back as he wraps an arm around my waist and kisses my shoulder.

"We will be fine, Denver," I whisper.

"I hope so, because the thought of losing you kills me."

"You won't lose me. Couples fight. We'll be fine."

"Get some sleep, baby." He pulls me even closer and wraps me in his warm, strong arms.

Chapter 22

Denver

I am waiting outside of Avery's last class of the day with her favorite coffee. This last week, since Kyle showed up, she has been distant. We are together every day and talking like normal. She insists I stay in her bed every night, but we haven't made love and she hasn't let me make her come since that night in the bathtub.

I know I handled things wrong, it's an adjustment being in a relationship after having no one to answer to but yourself for three years. I knew as soon as I threw that first punch at the punch bag that I shouldn't have walked away from her. I won't make that mistake again. I just need to get her to forgive me.

Students start exiting the classroom and I watch for her as I lean against the wall across from the door. When she sees me, her eyes light up.

I push off the wall and wrap her in a hug.

"Hey, baby." I kiss her forehead and hand her the coffee.

"Oh, perfect timing, I need this."

Once we are outside, I ask, "There's a football welcome back party tonight. Do you want to go? No crazy theme, just an excuse for a party."

She shrugs. "Sure, let's ask Kelsey, I'm sure she'll want to go too."

I hang out in their living room checking my social media while they get ready, then the three of us walk over together.

"Later, love birds." Kelsey waves and she disappears into the crowd, making Avery laugh.

I put my hand on her waist and guide her through the crowd toward the back room where I know the guys are hanging out. Halfway there, we get stopped.

"A-ver-E with a Y, not an E." Some drunk guy stops her, and she laughs. I might have tensed because she looks at me and smiles.

"This is Tom from my reading class. Tom, this is my boyfriend, Denver."

"Ahh, the reason she broke my heart. Nice to meet you, man." He tries to shake my hand, but I don't move my hands off of Avery.

"I don't know if I can say nice to meet you to a guy who just admitted to hitting on my girlfriend."

"Ah, she shot me right down, though." I fight a smile.

"Tom, how drunk are you?" Avery asks.

"Yeah, I've been here a while."

"Maybe it's best you go find a single girl tonight, don't waste your charms on me. There was a blond by the front door that looked lonely."

He mock salutes. "On it!"

"Well, he's fun," I say in her ear.

"He's harmless. I watched him hit on every girl until one gave into him the first day of class."

The whole team goes silent when they see me walk in with my arm around

Avery, then almost in unison they look over at Kyle at the other end of the room. I raise my chin and Avery raises an eyebrow at him and they stare each other down.

Kyle sighs and smiles then looks at the guys. "What? Avery can date whoever she wants."

Avery nods but everyone still looks wary and I know they are worried about what tension this could cause within the team.

"We already talked to coach, both of us. This issue is closed," I say with a stern voice, and within a minute everyone is talking again like nothing happened.

"Want anything to eat, baby?" I ask Avery.

"No, not yet, I was snacking during class."

"Want to dance?" I try to shift gears.

"You dance?"

I laugh. "Yeah, my mom taught me how to dance." I nuzzle my nose to her ear. "Lead the way."

As we get close to the dance floor, Sasha comes up and rubs her chest on my arm

—a classic Jersey Chaser move. She gives Avery a dismissive look and then pouts at me.

"Bolt, baby, won't you dance with me? You promised me a dance at the last party but then you disappeared."

I step away from her grasp and pull Avery closer to me, because dammit, this is the last thing I need with Avery already keeping me at arm's length.

"No, I blew you off at the last party. Don't call me baby, I'm not yours, never have been. I'm not interested in you or any of your pack. The only girl allowed to touch me or who I will be dancing with is my Avery. I've made that clear to you before." I'm being so loud that everyone around us has stopped what they're doing to watch.

"But you don't date." She eyes up Avery trying to gauge the competition.

"No, I didn't date because I was waiting on Avery. Even if she comes to her senses and dumps my ass tomorrow, I would never be interested in the likes of you, so stop wasting your time and leave me the fuck alone." I growl the last part out.

Avery wraps her arms around my waist and rests her head on my chest, which soothes my building anger. At that moment I don't care Sasha is there in tears and causing a scene.

"Come on, baby, I promised you a dance," I say, and lead Avery back to the dance floor.

Once we are on the dance floor, I lean to ear so she can hear me.

"I'm sorry about that."

"You handled it perfectly. It won't be the last time we deal with someone like her."

"I will make sure the word is spread so it is."

She smiles but turns and places her back to my chest and starts moving to the beat. Feeling her body move against mine is almost more than I can take. I take a deep breath, wrap my arms around her waist and start moving with her.

With Avery's ass moving against my cock to the beat of the music and her so close, I'm harder than I can remember being in a long time. I know she can feel me with every sway of her hips.

I lean my head down next to her just to take her in, her scent surrounding me causes everyone else around us to disappear. She leans her head back on my shoulder and closes her eyes with a smile on her face.

I kiss her neck, focusing on the soft spot below her ear and she reaches up to stroke my neck with her fingertips. I slowly trail my hands up her sides and cup her breasts.

I don't want to push her too far but the more she grinds against me the less I can keep my hands off her. I rub my thumbs over the peaks of her nipples, and she gasps in my ear, the sound alone is enough to cause me to groan.

She turns around and her eyes meet mine. I pull her hips to me and she wraps her arms around my neck, pressing her breasts to my chest. I wedge one of my thighs between hers and we keep dancing even as the song changes, but in this position, I know she is getting as worked up as I am.

I can see it in her eyes. I can tell by the way she is moving, and by how her breathing picks up. I rest my forehead on hers and close my eyes to just feel. I tighten the grip I have on her hips and move her a bit faster but when she gasps my name in my ear, I lose it and have to stop and take a step back.

"Want to go up to my room?" I ask her and she nods, breathing as heavy as I am.

I lead her to the stairs and up to the third floor where my room is. The one thing the football team did right is making the room like our own apartments. I barely get my key in the lock and the door open before she is pulling me in, and her lips are back on mine.

I kick the door shut behind us and spin her around and pin her to it in one move. Before all rational thought leaves me, I get the door locked.

Then I drop my keys and don't even bother with the light. I grab her ass and lift her so she can wrap her legs around my waist, but I don't move from the door. I know if I take her to my bed, I'm not going to be able to stop and she has been holding me at an arms distance until tonight, I don't want to push my luck.

A moment later her hands are on my chest and pulling my shirt off. *Tit for tat, baby*, I think as I remove her shirt and claim her lips again. Her hands are in my hair, pulling me close. I undo her bra and it joins the pile of clothes on the floor.

For the first time in a week, I can feel her skin to skin, and it goes a long way in calming my soul. I reach around and play with her breasts and pinch her nipples.

"Denver," she moans. "I want you so bad."

She reaches for the button on my jeans, but I grab her hands and hold them above her head, continuing to kiss her before I pull back and look into her eyes.

"Denver?" she whispers.

"Baby, I always want you, you will never have to wonder about that, but I need to know you've forgiven me. I know you've been keeping me at an arm's length, and I know I deserved it because I messed up, but I need to know we are okay before we fall into bed again."

She leans in and her lips ghost mine. "We're good, Denver. I didn't realize I was keeping you at arm's length until today. Seeing how loyal you were to me downstairs even through all this showed me what an idiot I've been. But we aren't going to fall into bed."

She senses my disappointment but quickly puts my mind at ease.

"You are going to take me right here against this door, do you understand?"

Holy shit! I almost come in my pants before I get a hold of myself. I set her down long enough to get both our pants and underwear off but the second I start to move toward my nightstand to get the new box of condoms I just bought, she stops me.

"Where are you are you going?"

"Condom," is all I manage to get out, but her grip still pulls me back.

"I'm on the pill and I was checked after everything back before Thanksgiving. I'm clean."

She is talking about her breakup with Kyle. My heart races.

"I haven't been with anyone in almost three years before you, and I get checked every year in my physical, I'm clean too. This is a big step, Avery."

"I know and I've never done this, but I want it, with you."

Taking my girl bareback. My heart is racing, and I can hear it beating in my ears. Even though she is on the pill I still need her to know.

"You know if anything happens, we are in this together, okay? You and me. I will always take care of you. I know you're on the pill, but I need you to know that," I tell her as I grab her ass and lift her up again.

I place my cock at her wet opening and almost lose it.

"I'm not even in you yet and it feels so good, baby, I'm not going to last."

"Denver," she moans, as she digs her heels into me, pulling me closer.

I thrust into her in one move causing her to cry out. I bury my head in her neck, trying to take it all in. How hot, soft, and wet she is wrapped around me. How tight she is and when she starts moving her hips, I move one hand down and stroke her clit because I need her there with me.

I thrust in and out of her, moaning with each stroke because it feels so damn good.

"God, baby, you feel like heaven." When I whisper in her ear, her pussy grips my cock, and I groan.

"Just like that, grip me tight so you feel every inch of me."

"I feel you," she gasps. "Oh God! Don't stop!"

She throws her head back and I know she's close. I pick up the pace and pinch her clit, causing her to cry out and clamp down on my cock as she starts to come.

"Just like that, sweet girl," I moan before I start coming too, releasing hot spurts of my come inside her. The thought of marking her makes me come so hard I see stars.

We are both trying to catch our breath, but since she still has her legs wrapped around me, I walk us to the bathroom and clean us both up before we crawl into bed. For the first time in a week, I get a good night's sleep.

Chapter 23

The last month has been busy. Kelsey has been dating a great guy, but that means she is never home, and over the last week Denver has canceled three out of four of our dates with not much of an explanation. But when he was over yesterday, he seemed tired and worn out. All he wanted to do was lie in bed watch TV and hold me.

Not complaining here, being in his arms in my favorite place to be, but my insecurities are starting to rear their ugly head. He isn't texting as much, even his good morning texts have stopped. Before I'd text him and unless he was at practice or with the team, he'd text me back almost right away. Sometimes now my texts go unanswered until the next day.

When I ask, he says he's been helping his mom with something but won't ever expand on what, saying he doesn't want to get me involved, or it's not his story to tell.

So, for these reasons, I'm pulling the emergency girls' night card with Kelsey. We don't do it often, but it means drop everything.

Me: SOS Emergency girls' night tonight.
Kelsey: I'll be there, what is going on?
Me: Something is going on with Denver, and I'm losing my mind, Kels.
Kelsey: I'll stop at the bakery. Class gets out in about thirty minutes, then I'm yours.

I'm already home in my PJs and on the couch with a glass of wine, and like the clingy girlfriend I am usually not, I give Denver one last ditch effort.

Me: I don't know what is going on with you, but I hate that you are shutting me out.

I set my phone down figuring like always he won't reply, and I go to fill up my wine glass. As I'm sitting back down my phone pings.

Denver: Baby, I just have somethings going on with my mom. I'm taking care of it then I'll be all yours again and I will make it up to you. Please wait for me.

I stare at my phone, wondering what the heck he means. Why doesn't he trust me enough to tell me what is going on? Is it something illegal? Would Denver do that? Would he cheat on me and try to cover it?

I must stare at my phone longer than I realize because he texts me again.

Denver: Avery, please, I'm asking for you to trust me. Please tell me you trust me, and you will wait for me.

Me: I'll try, Denver, but my heart hurts right now and I can't make you any promises.

Kelsey bursts through the door just then, pulling me away from the downward spiral I was in.

"Okay, I have cupcakes and wine. I told Ollie you pulled the SOS girls' night card when I canceled and he wanted to help, so he's bringing food over in a little bit and promised to drop and run, he wants to make sure you eat."

I wipe a few stray tears from my eyes. "Thank you."

"Give me five minutes." She runs to her room and changes into her PJs too, mandatory girl's night rules. Then she pours a glass of wine, grabs the cupcakes, and meets me on the couch.

"Okay, girl, spill it!"

"Everything was going great after the football party, then I thought it was in my head that he started to pull away, so I ignored it because he isn't Kyle, ya know? But the good morning texts stopped, then my texts go unanswered until the next day and he canceled the last three of our four dates with no explanation whatsoever. The one he did show up for he was tired, dark circles under his eyes and we just watched TV while he held me.

He's saying he's helping his mom with something but..."

I then show her the text messages she reads them and hands me back my phone.

"I try to tell myself he isn't Kyle, but it's starting to *feel* like that. Only, it didn't hurt with Kyle because I didn't care anymore. I didn't love him."

"Whoa, you guys dropped the L bomb?"

"Nooo!" I burst into tears and she climbs across the couch and wraps me in a hug.

"Your feelings are totally justified, babe, I say give him a bit more time. I don't know how much, only you know your limit. In the meantime, I promise to be around more. Ollie can cook, I'll make him our own personal chef. Tell me about your relationship before all this. Start when you got home from Christmas break."

So, I tell her about Denver's meeting with the coach, what happened after Denver bribed her out of the house for the night and the week following. I tell her about the football party and how loving he was after that. How he pampered me, and I hadn't ever felt so special and so loved but neither of us had said the L word. Then I go into how he started to pull away leading up to tonight's texts.

"What I don't get is that he says he waited so long for you, which is crazy romantic by the way, but now he doesn't trust you with what's going on? Any idea what it could be?"

"No, I talked to his mom last week and nothing came up. I couldn't bring myself to pry and worry her."

"When is the next time you are supposed to see him?" She hands me another cupcake and I dig in.

"Valentine's Day, he says he has something planned and I'm to wear a dress."

"Well, it could be that he has a huge surprise and he's working on it."

"I don't get that vibe, why ignore my texts? I know it sounds crazy but that's the one thing that always comforted me because it was consistent."

"It calmed your trust issues Kyle gave you. I get it. Well, how about this. Ollie and I had planned to do a Valentine's Day in, you know I don't like the hoopla behind it all. So, we'll plan it here at the house and make sure there is enough food for you, that way if anything happens you are here and it will be a friend-entine day, okay?"

I nod. "I know you two need your space, but it hurts too much to be alone. Though with how loud you are I'll take alone time hand down."

She bursts out laughing. "I'm not loud!"

"Come on, I'm still traumatized from your bar hook-up, sophomore year. Every time I hear, 'Spank me, daddy,' I have flashbacks. It was so loud I heard him spanking you."

We both erupt into laughter. That was the night we'd learned how thin the walls in the house are and had to make some new ground rules.

We spend the rest of the girls' night binging on sweets and wine until Ollie shows up. As promised, he drops off food, gives me a hug, kisses Kelsey on the cheek, and is back out the door.

"That man's a keeper," I say as I pull out our burgers, fries, fried chicken, biscuits, and pecan pie.

***

It's Valentine's Day and to say I'm nervous doesn't cover how I feel. Denver walked me to class this morning with coffee and a long-stemmed red rose. We were a bit early and our goodbye kiss turned into a bit of make out session before my professor walked by clearing his throat.

He was outside with lunch for me to walk me to my next class and laughed when I tried to guess what our plans are for tonight. He is acting normal, but he still has some dark circles under his eyes like he isn't sleeping. I wanted to ask, I wanted to push, but I didn't want to ruin today either, so I dropped it. He seemed relieved when I didn't bring it up too.

Now I'm home and getting ready for tonight. Kelsey and I have the radio cranked up as we do our hair and makeup. Ollie is coming over and staying here to be my back up plan and having them here makes me feel a bit better but with Denver's track record of canceling dates lately, I am just trying to stay positive.

The doorbell rings and I rush to answer it thinking it's Denver, but it's Ollie instead with bags of food in each hand.

It's then my phone goes off and my eyes meet Kelsey's and we both know. We just know what that text is. I want to ignore it because then I can pretend it's not real.

Denver: God, baby, you are going to hate me, but I have to cancel tonight. I swear it's for a good reason and I promise to tell you everything when I get back. Please, Avery, wait for me. Please.

CHAPTER 24

I toss my phone in the passenger seat and hit the steering wheel. I had the perfect night planned for us, for her, to show her how much I love her. I planned to tell her that tonight. It's cheesy I know It's been so hard not telling her.

Then my mom called. She's panicked. Her stalker seems to be back and making himself known around her house daily. It started with notes on her back porch, so I came down to secure the back yard with locks and motion lights. Then notes showed up on her car both at home and work. But when she got home tonight, he had been inside her house. Mom swears all the doors and windows were locked and closed which seems to only rile her up more. If I can't find someplace for her to stay, I'm going to make her take some time off work and come back with me. I can't leave her here alone after this.

I'm on my way to her now. I'm pissed the cops have done nothing to help my mom and I'm pissed this guy found her again. We thought he had given up after I moved her. I put the rental agreement in my name, and it's been quiet ever since.

I have an hour's drive and my thoughts get the better of me. I've canceled a few dates with Avery over the last couple of weeks and made the drive to my mom's when she was scared. I helped amp up her security, more locks, and some motion lights at her house and spent the night a few times when I didn't have early classes just to make sure she was okay.

I know Avery is hurting, I am too and it's killing me. I have to take care of my mom, I won't turn my back on her, but Avery means just as much to me. That's why I haven't told her what is going on with my mom. I don't want her mixed up with this and my mom doesn't want to worry her either.

In truth, I'm scared if Avery shows up at the house the guy will turn his attention on her as well. He's made it known he's been watching my mom with comments on how he like certain shirts she has worn or doesn't like others. Avery is a beautiful girl and who knows what this guy would do if he saw her. I can't let that happen.

Once I'm about twenty minutes out I call my mom again, but she doesn't answer and my stomach sinks. I try not to let the worst-case scenario enter my head, but this guy had been in her house. There were no signs of a break in, just a rose and his usual letter. My mom won't call the cops, they haven't even come out to take a report saying there is no threat the last three times she called. They came out the first two but still did nothing.

I don't know what I'm going to do, but she can't stay at the house any longer, and I can't go back to school until she is safe. I can't fix things with Avery until I can grovel face to face when I get back to school.

I pull up to my mom's house and my stomach sinks. The front door is open, and I don't even turn my truck off before I'm out and running up the front porch.

I'm barely inside the front door when I hear a male voice. I pull out my phone and dial 911. The second the dispatcher answers, I rattle off my mom's address and tell her a man broke in and is attacking my mom. I don't hang up I just leave my phone on the end table by the door.

The house is trashed, furniture flipped over, broken picture frames, and glass from the front window all over the floor. There is a hole in the living room wall and below it the coffee table is smashed up. The bathroom door is hanging off the hinges. I'd say a tornado went through here if I don't know any better.

The sounds are coming from the kitchen and I walk in and see my mom being pinned to the refrigerator by her throat.

"Get your hands off her," I yell, and move toward the man.

"I wondered how long before you got here." My father turns and sneers at me, and my stomach sinks.

"You've been doing all this?" I slowly make my way around the kitchen taking in my mom. She has a busted lip and a cut on her cheek, she looks terrified.

"Who else? You blew me off so easy I knew the best way to get your attention was through her. Of course, she was mine first. I thought I'd have some fun with her too."

"Put her down and let's talk this out, man to man."

He steps back from my mom but still has her pinned to the fridge by her neck.

"Nah, I think this is a good way to make sure you do exactly as I say." He tightens the grip on my mom making her eyes bulge and that's when I lose it.

I lunge for him and he so shocked he drops my mom who gasps for air and calls out my name. I land on top of my father on the floor and get one good punch in and hear his nose break and blood goes flying.

"Mom, go wait outside for the cops."

I don't have time to look up and make sure she goes before he lands a punch to my cheekbone. I'm almost double his weight, but it seems I've underestimated his strength. I won't do that again.

"You think you can run off and become this famous football star and not pay your dues to your own father? Not going to happen. You have half my DNA, so I say that means I get half the glory and money you make. "

"You get shit. You ran off before I was even out of diapers, you get exactly nothing." I land another good punch to the side of his face before he manages to get me off balance enough to roll us over, causing me to hit my head on the side of the counter.

He gets two more good hits to my face before I'm able to get my hands around his neck and slam him to the floor. In the distance, sirens ring out.

"You actually called the cops? You little shit." He starts to flail around more, trying to get away.

My guess is he probably has a few warrants out for his arrest and of course two new assault charges now. I sit on his chest while keeping my hands on his throat, silently enjoying his gasping for air like he made my mom do.

I don't move until the cops come running in, yelling at both of us to lie face-down on the ground with our hands behind our heads. I obey, but my father is stupid enough to think he can try to get out the back door. They have him tackled before he even gets it open.

"My mom, did someone get to her? Is she okay?" I ask as the events start to catch up with me.

"Yes, there is an ambulance on its way now. Are you Denver Bolter?"

Great just what I need for this to make the papers.

"Yes," I sigh.

"Sit up back to the counter I have to cuff you, per protocol," I nod and do as he asks. I answer all his questions and tell them about the stalking from the beginning and how many times I've moved my mom, how many complaints we tried to file, and how we couldn't even get a cop out to the house.

Another cop takes my mom's statement outside, but we aren't allowed to see each other. The cop in here with me tells me they are taking her to the hospital to check for internal injuries.

I rest my head back against the cabinet and close my eyes trying to keep the tears at bay. I don't care that my shoulders hurt from being pinned behind me. I care that my mom has to head to the hospital alone. I care that Avery is at home, hating me because I ditched her on Valentine's Day. I hate my father for all this.

I'm broken from my thoughts when the cop speaks.

"Listen, my old man used to wail on my mom when I was a kid and my family never did anything. It's why I became a cop, I wanted to help people. I just never realized how much my hands are tied by the law. It isn't always right. I'm a big MGU fan and I will work this case myself and do my best to keep it from the papers."

He uncuffs me and I rub my wrists and move my shoulders to work out the stiffness in them.

"On the record, I have to say you shouldn't have stepped foot in the house. You should have stayed on with the dispatcher and done as you were told. Off the record, I'm so damn proud of you for coming to stand up for your mother like that. Now I need to take you down to the hospital and have you checked out. That's not optional. I will take you in myself and straight to the back."

I just nod. He hands me his sunglasses, a hat I didn't notice him holding, and my cell phone before he guides me to the back of his car.

I foolishly check my phone, of course, there is nothing from Avery.

***

We ended up spending four hours in the hospital. I made them do every test in the book to make sure mom was okay and she insisted on the same for me. We both walked out with a bunch of bruises and scrapes.

Before we left, the cop who drove me to the hospital stopped in and said my father did have a warrant for his arrest on some drug and robbery charges. He was also being booked on double assault charges and I was cleared. He assured me again that he's doing his best to keep it all out of the papers.

At that moment I thanked him, but I couldn't care less. Mom is going to be okay, but my heart is bleeding over how Avery must be feeling right now. I should be worried about myself, but whenever I have a free moment, my brain goes back to her. I want to call her and beg her to forgive me, but I know she won't pick up and she deserves this face to face.

Thankfully one of mom's friends from work, Allie, is willing to let her stay at her place until mom's house is cleaned up. She picked us up and took us back to grab our stuff. They can carpool to work together and that makes me feel a bit better.

I'm helping mom pack when I look at her.

"Since you have Allie and are okay, I need to head back to school. I need to let coach know I won't make practice for a few days and I need to do it in person. I need to also apologize to Avery. "

"Baby, I am so sorry about all this. I am so thankful you were here, but I wish you had stayed at school and stayed out of all this. I don't like you driving right now, did you take the pain pill they gave you?"

"No, I'll take it when I get home. I promise I'll call when I get there."

She gives me the mom stare, but she can't change my mind. I need to get to Avery.

"Okay, you win that girl back, and let me know if I need to talk to her."

"Thanks, Mom." I hug her and head out.

The whole drive home all I can think about is how I'm going to win her back. I'm about twenty minutes from campus when the pain starts to really hit me. I know I can't go to Avery like this, I need to heal.

I head straight to my room take a pain pill and head to bed with the plan to talk to her in the morning.

Chapter 25

Avery

I spent Valentine's Day as the third wheel and drank way too many shots of vodka last night.

Ollie and Kelsey were so sweet. They tried to include me and kept the kissing to a minimum. I got so wasted that Ollie helped me to bed, made sure I took some aspirin and drank water.

It doesn't help that I still have a pounding headache which is only made worse when the front door slams shut. A moment later Kelsey comes bouncing into my room with a bag of tacos. My go-to hangover food.

Thank God.

She hands me more aspirin and water which I gladly take before scarfing down two tacos.

"How bad are you feeling?" Kelsey finally asks.

"Bad enough to skip class, but good enough to go pound down Denver's door and demand answers."

"Want some company?"

"No, just take some notes for me in class. I'm ahead on my work so I'm not worried about missing a day."

"I will be here for a girls' night tonight. I'm all yours. Ollie agreed."

"I owe that man, big time. Would it be weird to have you tell him his next orgasm was my thank you?"

"Yes! I'm not doing that!" She laughs.

"Yeah, I'm not thinking straight."

"Eat up, buttercup, go do your thing and take a nap. There are more tacos in the fridge for lunch, take some more meds with them."

I finish my morning tacos and get up and get ready. Nothing fancy, just sweats and a T-shirt and toss my hair up in a messy bun before I'm out the door.

I decide to walk to the football house. It's several blocks, but the cold fresh air is just what I need to get my brain clear before I talk to Denver.

I love him. I admitted it to myself last night and I know that is what is making all this even harder. It's making it hurt even more.

As I walk up the steps to the front door, Todd, one of the sophomore football players, walks out.

"Hey, Avery!"

"Hey, Todd. Is Denver in there?"

"I think he got in real late last night, so I doubt he will be going to class today."

I nod and thank him before making my way inside.

I say hello to a few of the other guys before heading to the third floor.

I stand outside his door for a minute and take a deep breath before and pounding my fist against it.

Nothing.

I pound again and this time there is shuffling on the other side, so I wait for him to open the door.

When he does, he takes my breath away. He's obviously sleeping because he's in just a pair of sweatpants, his hair is tousled, and he has stubble on his jaw. But what catches my eye is all the bruises. Black eyes, and marks on his chest.

"What the hell happened," I grit out.

He doesn't answer me at first, and I can tell by his shifty eye that whatever is about to come out of his mouth isn't going to be the truth.

"I was in a fight."

"And…"

He winces from pain or being caught in the lie, I'm not sure. My head hurts too much to try to figure it out, so I throw my hands up.

"It doesn't matter, I can't do this. I won't be lied to again. I'm done." I turn and start walking away.

"Avery!"

I don't even stop and turn around. I run down the stairs and out of the house, the cold air piercing my lungs.

Instead of heading home, I take the long way and head to my favorite burger stand and get the greasiest burger they have with extra fries. I walk a few blocks to a small park that is mostly empty and sit under a tree to eat.

I don't care how cold it is outside I just want to eat and be left alone. I finish off my burger as my phone pings.

Titan: Please tell me you made it home okay.

I'm not talking to him. Why does he care if I made it home when he hasn't cared what happened to me in weeks? I munch on my fries and watch a few people jog around the walking trail before my phone pings again.

Kelsey: Hey, I'm home from class, you okay?

Shoot, I've been sitting here for over an hour now. The cold that my thoughts have kept at bay slowly starts to seep in, so I stand up and start making my way home.

Me: Yeah, heading home now.
Kelsey: How did the talk go?
Me: He lied, I left.

I walk into the house and take off my shoes.

"Let me take a quick shower to warm up and get into PJs, then I'm all yours."

"Deal. Ollie wants to know if you want cupcakes or donuts?"

"Yes." I reply simply, unable to choose.

I hurry through a shower and getting dressed before plopping down on the couch just as Ollie shows up with donuts and cupcakes.

"You might as well stay and enjoy the Avery drama hour," I say to him, rolling my eyes.

He looks at Kelsey who shrugs. "I might need help getting her to bed again."

"Okay, let me know when you are hungry, pizza is on me tonight."

I recap my short conversation with Denver and the bruises on his face and ribs.

"A fight? You sure he was lying?"

"Yes, his eyes get all shifty and he makes this face. I know he was in a fight, but he wasn't willing to give me any details."

"No, that boy is crazy for you," Ollie chimes in.

We end up watching The Bachelor and playing a game Kelsey invented where we take a shot of wine every time, they talk about how much of a connection they have.

But the end of the night we are both pretty buzzed and once again Ollie helps me to bed, makes me take some aspirin and water before I pass out.

Chapter 26

I wake up and feel like utter shit. My body hurts, my head hurts, and my heart hurts, and I don't know which one is going to kill me today, but the pain from one surely will eventually.

When I got home from my moms, I took a painkiller and passed right out. I woke up around 6 a.m. used the bathroom and took another one.

Then Avery showed up. I was so out of it from taking the pain pill on an empty stomach I wasn't thinking clearly and answered the door with my bruises on full display. Then instead of telling her everything, I pushed her away.

This time I'm pretty sure I've pushed her away for good. There are only so many times you can mess up with a girl who has trust issues.

Well, my chance is completely gone.

When my head cleared yesterday, I went to talk to coach and explained what happened. He listened then lectured me for an hour on what I should have done, how I could have been hurt even worse, and how proud of me he was of me for protecting my mom.

I then confessed what had happened with Avery and his advice was to not back down but tell her the full truth. I plan to, if only I can get her to listen to me.

Then I got a call from my mom. Her landlord is pissed about the damage and doesn't seem to care that it wasn't her fault. He sees her as trouble and wants her out within thirty days. She isn't getting her security deposit back and there is barely enough saved to get her a new place. I don't know what to do but I need to figure something out fast.

I get up and head downstairs for some food. I need to get moving and back to normal. Today being Saturday I don't have any classes, so I'll hang out with the guys downstairs while I try to figure out my next steps.

Derick is in the kitchen when I come down and he sees me and hands me a plate with a few slices of pizza.

"So, I don't know if you are up for it but there is a party down on Greek row tonight, one of the sorority houses. No theme or dressing up required."

"No, as far as I am concerned, I'm still taken. I'm not going to some party."

"I knew you'd say that, but thought I'd offer anyway." Derick shrugs.

"Thanks, man, maybe we can go out tomorrow for a walk, I can't run yet but I need to keep moving."

"Let me know when and I'm there."

I spend the day playing video games before heading upstairs. I decided to skip the pain pills tonight and try to lie down in bed.

I'm thinking about Avery and our time over Christmas break, when Derick calls me. I can hear the noise of a party in the background, so I know he ended up at the sorority party.

"Hey, man, you need to get down here."

"I already said I'm not looking to get laid."

"Avery is here, and she's trashed, man."

My heart sinks. I know Avery isn't a party girl, so a Greek party is the last place I expected her to be tonight. I should have gone to her today, but I have no idea what I would have said or how to make things right.

"She with a guy?" I ask, praying like hell she's not.

"No, she is here with Kelsey and that guy she's seeing, but they have both been drinking too."

That's means there is no designated driver.

"Shit. Text me the address, I'm on my way."

Twenty minutes later I'm able to score a decently close parking spot and make my way in. I text Derick trying to find out where he saw her last, but I don't get a response, so I figure I'll start moving through the house.

This place is packed, even more so than the football parties because they let just about anyone in here, we are a bit pickier on who we let in the door to our parties. Not because we are snobs, but we try to keep out known troublemakers, and people who are known to bring drugs. We don't need that shit in the house.

I barely make it to the back of the first room before some blonde girl tries to pretend to fall into me.

"Oh!" She gives a fake giggle. "Sorry, too many people."

I remove her arms gently and push her away. Her mouth drops open, but I don't even let her speak.

"Not interested," I say and walk toward the kitchen without looking back at her.

I scan the kitchen and don't see Avery. I start to feel anxious and pray she is okay. I know so many guys like to pray on the drunk girls at parties like this. I swear I will rip off anyone's head who tries to touch her.

I make my way through the packed kitchen, shaking off a few more girls who try to grab on to me as I walk past and make my way to the dining room. I just walk in the door her voice filters through the air.

I'm relieved that I found her, but for only a minute, because when I find her leaning against the wall and some baseball player is pressed up against her. She has a cup of god knows what that is so easy to slip something into. I walk up and tap the kid on the shoulder, he isn't as tall as me and his eyes go wide when he sees me. I can't remember his name, I think it starts with an S, Steve, or Seth maybe.

"I suggest you get your hands off my girl," I tell him, and slide between him and Avery to dismiss him. I look at Avery who is smiling ear to ear.

"Denver! I'm so happy you're here," she slurs, and I wonder how much she's had to drink. To his credit, Seth or whatever his name is, walks away without another word and I take his place right in front of her, shielding her from the crowd.

"Baby, how many drinks have you had?"

"Umm, four or five?"

I take a deep breath. "This isn't you."

"It makes it hurt less."

"Makes what hurt less?"

"You."

"Avery..."

"Even with all the bruises, you are still the most beautiful guy I've ever seen," she says barely above a whisper.

I want to kiss her so bad, to hold her and tell her I love her, that she is the most beautiful girl even first thing in the morning when she is grumpy and sleepy. But I know this isn't the time.

"Well, we're even. I feel the same way about you."

She giggles and my heart sores at the sound. "I'm not a guy."

"No, but you are the most beautiful girl I've ever seen."

Her hand reaches out and lightly lands on my chest. I place my hand over it and soak in her touch. I know in the light of day when she is sober again, I won't get this chance.

"Let's find Kelsey and get you guys home. I want to make sure you get home safe."

"Such a knight in shining armor. They said they were going to head to the dance floor."

"Stay with me, okay?" I take her hand in mine and it tingles where we touch.

I lead her toward the den where the music is loudest, and a bunch of people are dancing. I scan the dance floor when Avery tugs on my hand. I look over at her and she points toward the corner. I follow her finger and see Kelsey sitting on Ollie's lap involved in a heavy make-out session.

I sigh. I hate to break up their fun, but Kelsey is important to Avery which makes her important to me and I will make sure she gets home safe too.

I approach and tap her on the shoulder "Kelsey."

She takes a minute before she pulls away and looks at me. She doesn't seem to be quite as drunk as Avery, but she definitely isn't sober.

"Come on, it's time to head home, how did you guys get here?"

"I drove them," Ollie says.

"And have you been drinking?" I ask him.

"Yeah, only two though, we're good."

"No way are you driving these girls' home. You take them to a party, I expect you to stay sober, that means not even one drink. You two abandoned Avery, she was cornered by some guy, anything could have happened there. Let's go, Kelsey, I'm taking you home, you can be mad at me tomorrow."

I hold out my free hand, not wanting to let go of Avery for even a second. Thankfully, Kelsey takes it and stands up. I take her hand in mine. "Do you girls need to grab anything? Coats or bags?"

They both shake their head, so I lead them to the door. The cold air hits me as we step outside and take in a deep breath. I still have to get them a good block down to my car, but at least they are out of there and safe.

Getting them into my truck is surprisingly easy as they both climb in the back seat and buckle up. I watch them in the rearview mirror on the way home and

Kelsey rests her head on Avery's shoulder and Avery stares out the window.

Not a word is spoken on the way home. I walk them to the door, but Avery has trouble getting her key in the lock. I reach over and help her then in a split moment decision I step inside to help her to bed.

"Kelsey, you need help to bed?"

"Nope, big guy, I'm good. Get her to bed and fix this shit, she has been drinking me under the table, I can't keep up." With that, Kelsey stumbles down the hall to her room.

I frown. This isn't the first night she has been drinking? That isn't like Avery. She will have a glass or two of wine, but she doesn't get drunk.

"Come on, baby, let's get you to bed." I wrap my hand around her waist and lead her to her room.

She sits down on the bed and I grab some pajamas. When I turn back around, she takes my breath away. She's taken her top off and is standing in just her bra and is attempting to remove her pants, but her balance isn't good enough.

"Here, baby, lie down and let me help."

She does and lifts her feet to me and I slowly pull down her jeans. I then slide on the pajama bottoms I pulled from her drawer and help her sit up so I can put her shirt on.

"No, get this off." She grunts as she tries to reach around and undo her bra.

This has to be a test and I feel like I'm going to fail miserably, there is only so much a guy can take. I'm at my limit when I unsnap her bra and she slips it off her leaving her breasts on full display.

I take a deep breath and pull her shirt down over her trying not to think about getting my mouth on them.

"Lie down. I'm going to get you some water."

"Need to use the bathroom." She stands and wobbles.

Once I see her make it to the bathroom safely, I head to the kitchen and get the aspirin and water and meet her back in her room.

"Take these, they won't stop the hangover you're going to have but they will help."

She takes the pills and drinks half a bottle of water before lying down. She scoots to the middle of the bed.

"Lie with me for a bit?"

I should say no but I can't, so I toe off my shoes and take off my jacket and lay down on top of the covers. I lie on my side, facing her but not touching her, and she is facing me.

"I'm so mad at you," she says, and my heart crumbles.

"I know, baby. I want to tell you everything, but not now, not like this."

"You've hurt me."

"I know, and that is the last thing I wanted."

"It's not fair."

"What isn't fair?

"How mad I am at you, but how badly I still want you."

"I'm yours, Avery. As far as I'm concerned, I'm still taken. That hasn't changed. We will get through this."

She yawns. "You still look really sexy, even with the bruises."

"You said that already."

"Will you kiss me?"

"Avery, baby, you're killing me. I want to kiss you, but you've had too much to drink and I'm not taking advantage of that. Next time I kiss you it will be because we've put this behind us okay?"

She closes her eyes. "Okay."

Less than a minute later her breath evens out and she is asleep. I should get up and head out, but I tell myself just a few more minutes. I want to watch her sleep and make sure she is okay because my gut is saying that I don't know when or if I will ever get this chance again.

I memorize every detail of her face, her scent, and even her breathing and commit it all to memory. The first rays of daylight start coming in the window when I finally pull myself from the bed and head out, locking the door behind me.

CHAPTER 27

Avery

I'm just getting home from my last class of the day when my phone rings. It's Denver again. He's been calling me every day for a week since the sorority party and I haven't picked up. I know it's the coward's way out, but if I talk to him, I know I won't be able to stay mad. I need to stay mad because I won't be lied to.

I can't deny what he did for me and Kelsey the night of the party. Making sure we got home okay. Once Kelsey found out Ollie had drunk and was planning to drive us home anyway, she dumped him. She wouldn't have drunk if he wanted to because we are very strict with each other and always make sure we have a designated driver.

I remember most of the night. Denver helping dress me and put me to bed, down to me asking him to kiss me and him saying no. He was gone when I woke up and I hate that I was disappointed. Then the calls started, I haven't picked up, but he leaves me a voice messages telling me he's sorry and that he wasn't thinking and asking if I'm okay. Still no sign of telling me the truth, though.

I take my stuff to my room and head to the kitchen to figure out dinner when Kelsey comes flying in.

"So, Ollie wants to meet for dinner to apologize and explain, he is taking me to that fancy steakhouse we were talking about the other day. I'm going to let him, cause, hey, a girl has to eat, right? I'm driving. Will you be okay tonight?"

"Yeah, I'm good. I've got some reading for school to do. Make sure you order an appetizer and dessert!" I yell after her.

She emerges a few minutes later in a nice dress that will make Ollie swallow his tongue.

"I also plan to order the biggest steak on the menu." She sits next to me on the couch and sighs. "I really like him, ya know? I was ready to be serious with someone for the first time in a long time."

"Then hear him out. And go with your gut and I'm here if you need a ride."

"You should call Denver and see what he wants at least."

"Yeah, maybe."

She rolls her eyes then heads out the door. I decide to warm up the leftover pizza from last night and snuggle in to watch a few movies that have been on my to watch list for far too long. I'm about halfway into the first one when the doorbell rings.

There stands Denver looking almost as bad as the morning I showed up at his room. I go to close the door in his face, but he stops it.

"I really did get into a fight," he says. I study his face and I can tell this time he's telling the truth.

"Ready to tell me the whole truth?"

"Yes, every detail."

I open the door and let him in. He heads to sit on the couch, I turn the TV off and shoot a quick text to Kelsey asking her to take her time. I sit down on the love seat and look at him. He has his elbows on his knees and his head in his hands staring at the floor.

"I got into a fight with my dad."

Shit, that isn't what I was expecting. I move to sit next to him, hesitantly reaching out start rubbing his back.

"My senior year of high school I started to make a name for myself after I got a scholarship. I broke up with my girlfriend because she turned from a caring girl to a Jersey Chaser looking for a free ride almost overnight. It was also when my dad showed up out of the blue, thinking he could cash in on a free ride too. When we didn't let him, he left. I thought that was the end of it. My mom didn't tell me over the summer that weird things started happing. It started with cute notes left on her car, flowers at her door, then it got creepy. The first night we met it was her calling me because she was so freaked out. I drove home and we moved her out of the apartment trying to get her away from her stalker. I put her apartment in my name so he couldn't find her."

He pauses, taking a few deep breaths. "We thought it was over. Then on Thanksgiving my dad showed up. Wanted me to sign some stuff so he could sell it to some of his buddies for cash, he said I owed him that. I refused and told him he owed my mom back child support. He threw a fit and left. After Christmas break, the letters started again. The cops wouldn't do anything because there were no threats. Notes left for her on her car at work talking about things like what she ate for dinner the night before. Notes left at home talking about how he liked what she was wearing. Every evening I could get home, I went, helping her secure the house with better locks etc. It's not in the best part of town as you know, and I could tell she was scared."

"Denver..."

"Let me get this out, please."

I nod.

"Then on Valentine's Day, I was getting ready to head out to pick you up and she called. She got home and there was nothing out of place, but she found another letter inside the house, on her kitchen counter. I dropped everything and headed to her. I texted you while I was on my way. I got there and the front door was open and there was glass everywhere. I called 911 and gave them her address and went inside. She'd struggled hard. Doors off the hinges, overturned and broken furniture and holes in the wall. I found her in the kitchen being pinned to the fridge by my dad."

"No," I barely whisper. Tears are running down my face, but I wipe at them, trying to stay strong for him.

He nods. "First chance I got I lunged at him and told my mom to meet the cops out front. We rolled on the kitchen floor and he got in some good punches, and by the time the cops showed up I had him pinned to the ground. He admitted the letters were to scare both of us and went on and on about how I owed him. Thankfully one of the cops took pity on me and is doing his best to keep this out of the media. I told coach about it too. But that night after we got out of the hospital, I took her to pack up some of her stuff and she was able to stay with a friend from work. I came home took a pain pill the hospital gave me and passed out. I remember waking up and taking another pill in the morning not too long before you got there. All I remember thinking was that I didn't want any of this to touch you. I wanted to show you I could handle this so you knew I was someone who could take care of you. But I don't remember what I was thinking the morning you showed up. I was so out of it, Avery."

I keep rubbing his back. "I would have understood from the start. I would have been at the hospital with you, I would have helped, if you had let me."

"Avery, the landlord is kicking her out, says she is too much trouble and wants her gone by the 14th of next month. She isn't getting her deposit back, my dad's in jail but he found her this time and could find her again when he gets out. I don't know what to do."

Then this big strong guy in front of me breaks down crying and it rips my heart out. I wrap my arms around him and pull him into me and he buries his face in my neck.

"I can't lose you too, I'm going crazy. I can't eat or sleep. Please tell me what to do, how to fix this," he sobs.

I pull away slightly, but he won't look at me. I move down to the floor and kneel in front of him and frame his face with my hands, bringing his gaze up to look at me.

In his eyes, in that moment, I know. Even though he lied to me, I trust this man with everything I am. The way he came and took care of me at the party, the way he handled the Jersey Chasers after Christmas break, the way he didn't think twice about coming to help me on Christmas break, and how much he cares about his mom. This man is my everything.

"All I wanted was for you to talk to me instead of shutting me out. I don't want to be lied to. I want you to lean on me, let me support you and help you like you have me."

He wipes his face on his sleeve then puts a hand behind my neck and pulls me in for a kiss. It's so soft and unsure, but as soon as I kiss him back, his other hand comes up to my cheek and he takes control and deepens this kiss. His tongue running along mine and I try to convey in that kiss what he means to me.

He pulls back slightly and whispers along my lips. "I love you, Avery."

Those words seal this moment for me. I know this is it. I smile, "I love you too, Denver."

CHAPTER 28

Denver

My heart stops. This amazingly beautiful girl loves me back. After all this time, all the pain of waiting up to this moment, and I know I'd do it all over again. Well, not the not telling her about my mom part but the rest of it.

"Say it again, sweet girl," I say, my voice raw with emotion.

"I love you, Denver."

"God, I love you too." I slam my lips back to hers and without breaking the kiss she climbs into my lap, her legs straddling mine and for the first time in weeks, I forget about everything. The stress with my mom, her landlord, all of it, and I lose myself in Avery.

"Wrap your arms around my neck and hold on tight," I whisper against her lips.

I don't let her speak before my lips are back on hers and I grip her ass and stand up. She wraps her legs around my waist as I take her to her room and kick the door closed behind me. I'd take her right there on the couch, but I don't want to chance Kelsey and her boyfriend walking in, because no one gets to see my girl like this but me.

"Please tell me you haven't been drinking tonight," I murmur as I lay her down on the bed.

"Not a drop."

"Thank Christ." I reach over and pull her shirt and bra off, because after the party all I could think about were these breasts. They stared in every dream I had. I take them into my hands and give them a firm squeeze, causing her to moan.

I suck and nip at her already hard nipples before sitting up to remove my shirt and then sliding off her pants and underwear. Seeing her completely naked on the bed in front of me with a light flush on her face has me so hard. I take a deep breath. This is me showing her how much I love her.

So, I pull her to the edge of the bed and kneel on the floor in front of her as I spread her legs wide. I can see she is already wet for me and I lean in and run my tongue along her slit, sucking hard on her clit.

"Denver!" she yells my name, making me smile.

"I love it when you're loud for me, baby. It lets me know how much you love it."

Pushing her legs even further part, I start making love to her pussy with my mouth. A few hard sucks on her clit is all it takes to send her over the edge screaming my name and putting the biggest smile on my face.

I stand up and quickly undress as she scoots back up the bed. I can't take my eyes off of her. I climb onto the bed and smile.

"On your hands and knees, sweet girl."

I watch her eyes go wide and she doesn't move.

"You trust me?" I ask.

"More than you know."

"Then get on your hands and knees for me." This time she is up and in position with her perfectly round ass facing me. I scoot in behind her and run my hand up her back. When she looks over her shoulder at me, I almost lose it. Real life Avery is better than any imagination I could dream up.

I line my cock up at her slit and her warmth has me moaning. I get a firm grip on her hips and fill her with one firm thrust, causing her to cry out.

I set a slow and steady pace and slide my hand from her hips up her belly to her breasts. I lean over her and pinch her nipples and her pussy flutters around me.

"I missed this so much, baby. This is my safe haven right here inside of you," I murmur into her neck.

She gasps and I can tell she is close. I pull her up, so she is up on her knees seated on my lap, my cock fully inside her and her back to my chest. She throws her head back on my shoulder and I slide a hand down to her clit and start rubbing it.

Having her skin to skin is sending my body into overdrive.

"I love you so much, baby. I'm going to spend the rest of my life proving it to you, making you proud. It's you and me against the world from now on."

"Denver..." she moans. "I love you too."

In that moment I pinch her clit and she shatters in my arms. I only get a few more thrusts in before I start coming inside her, coating her, and marking her once again as mine.

When my balls are finally empty, I lay us both down and she turns to rest her head on my shoulder and wraps an arm around my chest. I slip out of her.

We lie there just soaking each other in, as I run my hand up and down her back, just wanting to enjoy this moment of her in my arms.

"I have an idea for your mom," Avery says, breaking the silence.

"I'm open to anything, because I'm out of ideas."

"Well, I know a nice old empty house in Nashville that needs a little love."

"Avery..." I whisper her name.

Is this girl suggesting what I think she is?

"I never rented it out and I don't need the money. She could work it off by helping repaint and redecorate the place. I had an alarm system put in right after we left for Christmas break. Mr. Burns was there with the guy for me. There is no chance of her getting kicked out, I heard the landlady is pretty cool. I know the neighbors love her and would help watch out for her. Yard work is taken care of including shoveling snow. I know it's far from her job, but with no rent maybe she could get her foot in the door at a décor firm?" She shrugs like it's no big deal. This is a huge deal.

"You mean it?"

She props her head up on her elbow and looks down at me. "Of course, I mean it. We can move her in this weekend, and I want to call my dad about her current landlord, I'm pretty sure he can put some heat on him and she might even get her security deposit back, seeing how this wasn't her fault."

I roll her over and kiss her, because I have no words.

Chapter 29

Once Denver and I had a plan for his mom, it took a little convincing to get her on board. She said she was sad to leave her job because she really liked her boss. She was worried because she would be giving up her benefits. She and Denver had a heart to heart that night about the talks with the NFL and how he plans to take care of her no matter what.

In the end, she couldn't pass up the opportunity to help with the house. When I started talking about using it to launch her interior decorating career, her eyes light up and I know that didn't escape Denver either.

The next battle I had was them letting me hire movers. They refused and we went back and forth before they let me rent a Uhaul truck and they got a bunch of guys from the football team to help.

So that's where we are. It's been two weeks since I made the suggestion she move into my house and today is moving day.

When Denver went to his coach and explained his plan asking to miss a few days of training and offering to do double the work when he got back, the coach refused to make him train double then offered guys to help him move and take the weekend off from training. So now there are ten bulky football guys plus Denver in and out of Gina's house, helping pack up the last of it.

One guy turned out to have worked on his dad's construction crew growing up and is fixing some of the damage so less will come out of her pocket at the end.

Gina and I are currently outside sitting on the tailgate of Denver's truck watching the guys move her couch into the truck.

"If I was ten years younger." She sighs and shakes her head, causing me to laugh.

"There are advantages to dating a football guy but there are disadvantages too. Do you know how much he eats?"

Gina laughs. "I used to cook for him in high school, when he hit a growth spurt, I couldn't keep enough food in the house, he would eat anything and everything. I caught him eating a raw potato once when I got home from work because there were no clean pots to cook it in. He got a hard lesson on doing dishes that day."

We are both laughing when Denver steps out of the house with a huge smile on his face.

"This is what I like, to see both my girls smiling, happy, and safe." He kisses his mom on the cheek and gives me a chaste kiss on the lips.

Just then, a black expensive-looking car pulls up on the curve.

"Who is that?" I ask.

"He wouldn't," Gina whispers, and the smile falls from Denver's face.

A well-dressed man steps out. He looks to be in his mid 40s with dark brown hair which is greying at the temples. He is wearing jeans and a sweater, but you can tell with just one look they are expensive.

"Mom, who is that?"

"Clint, my boss. Well, ex boss."

I've recently learned when Gina says her boss, she means the owner of the whole company. That makes sense, he just oozes money. We all watch him look up at the house then when his eyes land on Gina his whole face softens, and he smiles as he walks over to us.

"Oh shit," I say, and Denver's eyes snap to me.

"Clint, what are you doing here?" Gina asks as he gets closer, but she makes no move to get off the tailgate and Denver acts as a bit of a buffer between her and him, which makes me smile.

"I get back from a week of meetings and find out you quit," he states with no emotion on his face. I have to stop myself from rolling my eyes and saying, no shit, Sherlock.

"I did."

Clint smiles at Gina again. "That means you no longer work for me."

"Does it now? I had no idea." Gina manages to keep a straight face, but it doesn't take a blind man to see what's going on and I can't help but burst out laughing.

"You're moving?" he asks.

"No, we just thought we'd load up all my stuff and take it for a drive then put it all back," Gina sasses back.

At this point, I can't stop laughing so I slide off the tailgate and walk up to him.

"I'm Avery, Denver's girlfriend. You have an uphill battle here, try being more direct."

He shakes my hand. "You wouldn't be willing to help me out, huh?"

"She's moving to Nashville."

"Why?"

"Uhh..." I look back at Gina, who is giving me her 'don't you dare' mom face.

"I guess the answer depends on you. Why are you here?" Gina asks.

I move over and loop my arm into Denver's. "Maybe we should give them some privacy." I try to tug Denver's arm.

"Don't move," Gina says, and we freeze.

Then she sighs. "I quit because I'm being forced to move out of here.

Denver's father was leaving weird notes and gifts around the house, I didn't know it was him, the cops didn't do anything, then Valentine's Day he broke in, trashed the place bad, you can go in and see for yourself. The landlord wants me out, gave me thirty days."

I watch the anger cross Clint's face.

"Why didn't you tell me?"

"Why would I? You're my boss, not my therapist."

"What happened to his father?" Clint asks through gritted teeth.

"He's in jail."

"This isn't the first time this happened, she had to move a few years back too," I say, and Gina shoots me a death glare. "Okay, shutting up now."

I try to pull Denver away and he still won't budge, but this time he puts his arm around my waist and tucks me into his side. When he kisses the top of my head, I just wrap my arms around his waist.

"Why Nashville?" Clint asks.

When no one answers, I sigh. "My grandma passed away over the summer and left me her house. I grew up there and plan to keep it but still have another year of school and it needs some work. Mostly painting and redecorating. Gina is moving in there to help me out. She has always wanted to do interior decorating and I loved her ideas when she came up with me over Christmas break, so it was a perfect fit."

Denver squeezes my hip and his mom shoots me a stern look, one my mom used to give me when she wanted me to stop talking.

"Listen, apparently I'm the only non-blind person here, stop giving me the death glare. Christ, Clint, put us out of our misery before they kill me" I give him a glare.

"Won't kill you, sweet girl, but you will pay later," Denver finally speaks.

Clint takes another step toward Gina, and Denver steps to the side to allow him.

"I wish you'd told me what was going on, I would've helped. The thought that you were scared kills me. I should have paid better attention."

"Maybe secure your parking lot?" I suggest.

"What?" Clint asks.

"Some of the notes were left on her car while she was at work," I tell him.

"Avery..." Denver growls.

"What? He can make it safer for his employees, he should know." I shrug.

Clint rubs the bridge of his nose. "You should have reported that to me, Gina," he says softly. "You know I value everyone's safety there."

"The cops said it wasn't threatening, why would I have thought you'd believe any differently?"

It's then Clint laughs and it's a full laugh. "Guess I was better at hiding my feelings then I thought."

"Ya think?" I laugh.

Then he rolls up his sleeves and holds up his arms. "Well, I'm here, put me to work."

Gina's jaw drops causing me to laugh.

This time when I pull Denver away, he comes with me.

"They are so cute," I sigh.

"You are in so much trouble," he growls into my ear.

"I'll gladly take any punishment you dish out, it's obvious Clint cares for your mom and has been hiding it because she worked for him. She quit and now he's here to make his move. He isn't happy that she is moving, but I have a feeling he will find a way to make it work."

Denver's eyes go wide, and he looks back at his mom and Clint who are smiling at each other before he sighs. "If it had to be anyone, I'm glad it's him. He's loaded so I know he can take care of her, plus he's always been really nice to both of us."

We finish packing before lunch and then the great debate comes over who is riding with who. Clint wants to drive Gina, but she needs to take her car. I suggest one of Denver's teammates drive it, since the ten of them came in two cars I'm sure they would be grateful for a bit of space.

Denver is driving the moving truck and wants me to ride with him. I laugh. "No way, because I am driving your truck. Derick said he'd ride with me."

That earns Derick a scowl from Denver and after some hushed whispers Denver agrees. I make sure everyone has the address and we all head out.

Once we hit the interstate, I glance over at Derick.

"I get a feeling you volunteered to ride with me because something is on your mind, so let it out."

"You know Denver has liked you for a while," he says.

"I wasn't aware until recently, but yes, I know now."

"I've never seen him so down as the week you broke up. If I didn't make sure he was eating dinner, I don't think he would have eaten at all."

"He lied to me," is all I say.

"I know, he told me the full story. Not saying he didn't deserve it. Guess I'm botching up my words. I don't do this romance shit."

"Well, I don't need it sugar coated, just spit it out." I laugh.

"Listen, I know what Kyle did to you. I didn't agree with it, but coach has this thing about team loyalty. It tore Denver up watching it and I'm guessing he found a way to get you to that party that night." He laughs. "Denver isn't like Kyle. I can vouch he was never once into the Jersey Chaser scene; he always went home alone, and I've seen him make more girls cry for trying to climb into his lap than I can count. You have been it for him since freshman year, I know the whole story, he's told me."

I sigh. "I wish I had known."

"Listen, this is my long and drawn out way of saying Denver is one of the good ones, treat him right or you will have the whole football team to deal with, but many of us were talking after it came out that Kyle had grabbed you and we decided team unity only goes so far. If he hurts you, really hurts you, you let us know and we will take care of him."

I give him the side eye. "Aren't you his best friend? Shouldn't you be on his side no matter what?"

"I am his best friend and that means he ever puts his hands on you I will beat the shit out of him. A few guys had our way with Kyle on and off the field after it came out that he grabbed you and left a bruise. Denver refused to do it because he knew Kyle would go to coach and try to make it look like he was causing problems for stealing you."

"Kyle did go to coach, then ambushed me at my place later that afternoon. Thankfully, Denver was there but that was our first fight for the way he reacted after Kyle left."

"I was in the gym, I heard it all while he beat the shit out of the punching bag."

"I'm not going anywhere," I sigh as I pull up to the house. I park on the road knowing Denver will want to back the truck into the drive.

"Good. Which one's yours?" he asks. I get out and he follows me up the front door as head up to unlock the house.

"This is your house?"

I cringe waiting for it. I don't tell people I have money because they tend to treat me differently, thinking either that I think I'm too good for them or they see me as an ATM and meal card.

But throughout the day, not one of the guys treats me any differently. As the guys are unloading and helping move Gina's stuff in, Clint comes up to me in the kitchen where I'm making some sweet tea.

"I ordered pizza for the guys, it's past lunchtime."

"Thank you, Clint."

He nods and leans against the counter.

"This was your grandma's house?"

"Yeah, I grew up here. It was too hard to come back until Gina and Denver came with me over Christmas break. Having them here it felt like home again."

"When did you put the alarm system in?" he asks.

"January of this year. Mr. Burns next door oversaw it. They are good friends of the family. His son is in high school and does all the landscaping here. I talked to him about making sure the drive and all is shoveled if it snows, so Gina doesn't have to do it. They will also keep an eye on her."

"Good."

"You going to ask her out or not?" I get right to the point.

"Don't beat around the bush, do you?"

"Nope. I'm not her daughter, but the first time I met her Denver was rescuing me from a bad blind date and he took me home to his moms and she made fried chicken. She treated me like I was family ever since. I'm protective of her and have no plans of going anywhere."

"Been looking to expand the offices a bit. Was looking at Knoxville, but I think Nashville has potential."

Just then Denver walks in and wraps his arms around me, ignoring Clint.

"Nashville does have potential. It's the state capital, they have a good airport, country music, good food, all things Johnny Cash." I smile.

He smiles too. "And now Gina." He nods. "Denver, can I talk to you?"

I laugh and head out to help Gina unpack.

Later that night, lying in bed with Denver, he sighs. "Clint asked my permission to date my mom."

"Did you give it to him?" I ask.

"Yeah. They have a date next week."

"Good. I like him."

"A little too much," he grumbles.

"You know my comment wasn't because of his looks, it was because I saw his face when he looked at your mom, it's the same one you give me. I knew then."

He leans up on his elbow and looks down at me.

"What look do I give you?"

"Like I'm your whole world. How much you love me is written all over your face in that one look."

"Because you are my whole world, sweet girl, my everything, always." He mummers before his lips land on mine.

Epilogue

2 years later

The crowd goes wild as Denver completes another touchdown. As always, he looks back toward my seat, places his hand over his heart then kisses his hand and points to me. He does this at every game now, home or away.

The sports guys on ESPN love it, and it's made girls everywhere go crazy for him. Neither of us likes that last part, but he does it for me, and that's all that matters.

It's been an eventful two years since the day we moved Gina into my house in Nashville. Clint opened up a Nashville office and they started dating. He treats her like gold and just asked her to marry him over Christmas this year. He took her to a cabin in Gatlinburg for a weekend. She said yes and has been smiling much more.

I look over at them now. The three of us haven't missed a game of Denver's since he was drafted first round to the Tennessee Titans. Clint insisted on making sure we had seats for every game. He wanted to rent out a VIP box at every stadium, but Gina and I put our foot down unless the weather is really bad. Like when they played the Green Bay Packers in Wisconsin in December.

It's a good thing I can write anywhere. When Denver found out I wanted to write books, he insisted I do it, he wanted me to be happy. So, I wrote a romance novel based on our story, called *Just One Kiss*. It sold like crazy and made the best seller's list. Then I let leak that it was based on our story and it went crazy again.

I couldn't get another book out fast enough, but book two just released last week and it's based on Gina and Clint's story. They loved that I wanted to write it and I've donated the proceeds to the charity Denver and I started.

His first year on the team he has earned his nickname the Lighting Bolt and fans have gone crazy over it. There are T-shirts and everything. When the name gained popularity, we partnered with the team and made some Lightning Bolt merchandise, and all the proceeds go to help single moms with everything from food and bills to helping put them and their kids through college.

Our last year of school we took a leap of faith and Denver moved in with me and Kelsey over the summer. We hadn't spent a night apart, so it just made sense. It worked out really well because Gina visited more and cooked for us a lot.

Kelsey and I are still best friends. She lives here in Nashville and has been dating one of Denver's teammates for the last year. It seems to be pretty serious. She was pissed when on graduation day I gave her back the money she had been paying in rent.

I told her she needed to use it for a place to stay when she got a job and I wasn't taking no for answer. She agreed, but for the last year every time we meet for our weekly lunch date, she insists on paying.

As the NFL draft got closer Denver got more and more nervous. Finally, I had to sit down with him and explain that it was a good thing that so many teams were talking about him and I had every intention of going wherever he did, and his mom could stay in my house.

When he realized we wouldn't be apart no matter where he ended up, he calmed down. When he was drafted to the Titans, he fell to his knees and almost cried. When he was asked about his reaction in an interview later, I will never forget his response.

"My mom was a single mom and busted her butt to raise me, sometimes working two jobs just so I could play football. In that moment, knowing I could flip the tables and finally take care of her was everything I had ever dreamed of."

Another interviewer asked what the first thing he bought with his signing bonus was.

"I bought my mom her own place, a new car, and took her and my girl shopping. I spoiled them both."

Not too long after that, some rumors started to fly that I was with Denver for his money and had leeched on to him for his climb to fame. He was pissed, and while I said to just ignore it, he made it known that I had my own money and no reason to want his. He was pissed about the media attack on me and made it clear to any news outlet who went after me or his mom that he would refuse interviews and would file charges against.

The fans went crazy with how protective he is. When Gina moved into her new place, Clint grumbled that he wanted her to move in with him. She said his penthouse was too big and if he wanted them to live together, he could move in with her and live more simply or deal with it.

Clint had them both moved into her place the next day. He has also helped her with her interior design business. He does real estate and conveniently started in the housing market when he moved to Nashville, so he's hired her to stage all his homes for sale and decorate his rentals. Rentals he rents out to single moms at a hugely reduced rate.

He works with the women's shelters and he won't admit it, but I know there is one mom who is eighteen, her parents kicked her out because she is pregnant, and he made her a deal. She could live there rent free as long as she graduated high school and got a college degree. I also know he is paying for the degree even though he won't admit it. Clint is a big ole softy he just doesn't let anyone who isn't close to him see it.

Things with Denver and I have been amazing. He moved into Grandma's house with me and we made it a home. Gina did a great job decorating it, Denver added a killer outside kitchen and seating area complete with an outdoor TV. He's trying to convince me to allow him to add a pool, but we settled for a hot tub for now. He did insist on a few more security features such as a fence all around the property, including a front gate.

I agreed so long as we could still do all the Christmas lights. The house is set back far enough that we can still put the lights up and be seen but have our privacy from people on the street.

Denver has gained popularity in the NFL real quick. He's scored more touchdowns than anyone this year and is the reason the Titans are playing in the Super Bowl today.

Denver and Clint banded together and insisted we share a VIP suite with some other families from the team for safety reasons, so we agreed. He also agreed with Clint on getting us each a security detail while at the stadium today. They are both overprotective. My mom and dad are also with us today. They already consider Denver their son and have made it to many of his games especially the away games because it meant they would be traveling.

They are now in the last sixty seconds of the game and I turn to Mom, Dad, Clint, and Gina.

"I can't stay here!" I get Rob's attention, my bodyguard, as I call him and head down to get as close as I can to the Titan's side of the field. Titans are up by seven points, but Dallas has the ball. All they have to do is stop them from scoring, but if I know my Denver, that won't be enough.

It happens so fast I don't see it. One minute Dallas is supposed to have the ball and the next Denver is pulling away from the crowd running toward the end zone faster than I've ever seen him run. I know he has the ball without having to see it, but I know the moment the crowd does, and the Tennessee fans go crazy. Thirty yards, twenty yards... I don't realize I'm holding my breath. Ten yards... touchdown! I'm yelling right along with the crowd.

Denver grabs his chest then points to the VIP box where he thinks I am and whips off his helmet as the team rushes him. He just won the Super Bowl for his team. Even if the kicker botches the field goal, which I know he won't, they've won.

Denver runs over for some water and I know the moment he sees me because he changes course and pulls me over the fence and onto the field.

"We did it, baby." He kisses me, but I pull back.

"Denver, *you* did it."

"No, this was us, everything that happens on that field is us, because you support me, you haven't missed a game, you deal with my crazy schedule and love me through it all, so *we* did it."

He kisses me again and I don't realize we are moving until he sets me down and I see we are at the fifty-yard line. He tucks some hair behind my ear and smiles at me.

"I knew freshman year you were it for me. One kiss is all it took. That second kiss? I knew we'd be here one day, no matter how long it took." He smiles, and his coach walks up and takes his helmet, and shakes his hand. He walks back off without a word and it's then I realize how many eyes are on us. His whole team is lined up watching on the sideline.

"Eyes on me, sweet girl," he says. I look back at him and when his eyes meet mine, he drops to one knee and it's then I realize what's happening.

"I dreamed of this day, winning the Super Bowl, since I started playing football. Since freshman year I dreamed you'd be at my side when I did. When the day it was announced we'd be here, I knew that win or lose, I'd be right here after the game. I love you, Avery Jessa Hayes, with my whole heart. Your support is the reason I'm here today; I know I couldn't have done this without you. I want to spend the rest of my life with you by my side. I want to wake up at 3 a.m. and find you writing because an idea came to you, I want to know you are always in the stands, I want to convince you to let me put a pool in our back yard, I want to have kids and watch them grow up in that house like you did. But most of all? I want to go to sleep every night with you in my arms and wake up the same way. Will you do me the honor and be my wife?"

A hush falls over the crowd, but I don't see any of them, all I see is my future down on one knee offering me the life I always dreamed of.

"Yes!"

His team roars, as does the crowd. Denver slips the ring on my hand as his team circles around us cheering. It's a day we won't ever forget.

Later that night at the hotel suite Denver got us, we are taking a bath together, my back to his chest just soaking everything in.

"What kind of wedding have you always dreamed of, sweet girl?" Denver asks me has he runs his hand up and down my sides and kisses my neck.

"I think we should do something small, just family a few close friends but a destination wedding."

"Is that what you always dreamed of?"

"As a kid, I thought I'd marry a prince and have a big Princess Diana wedding. I'm not quite into that anymore. But I think we should get married soon before I start to show..." I have to bite my lip. His hands stop and he sucks in a breath.

"Avery?"

"You're going to be a daddy. I found out this morning just after you left."

His hands smooth over my stomach and his face is in my neck. A few tears run down my shoulder.

"God, I love you Avery, so damn much. I didn't think there was anything better than you agreeing to be my wife today, but you managed to find it. I promise to spend the rest of my life taking care of both of you."

"And we will spend our lives taking care of you too."

***

Want more long time crushes turning into sexy romances? Check **out She's Still The One.** A brother's best friend, rock star romance with all the feels!

***

Want more second chance romances? Check out **The Cowboy and His Best Friend** and **Sunset**.

***

Get 2 free books. Join Kaci Rose's romance-only newsletter to get free books, subscriber only deals, and stay up to date with the newest releases.

Join Kaci Roses Newsletter Here.

See All of Kaci Rose's Books

Oakside Military Heroes Series
Saving Noah – Lexi and Noah
Saving Easton – Easton and Paisley
Saving Teddy – Teddy and Mia
Saving Levi – Levi and Mandy

Chasing the Sun Duet
Sunrise
Sunset
Rock Springs Texas Series
The Cowboy and His Runaway – Blaze and Riley
The Cowboy and His Best Friend – Sage and Colt
The Cowboy and His Obsession – Megan and Hunter
The Cowboy and His Sweetheart – Jason and Ella
The Cowboy and His Secret – Mac and Sarah
Rock Springs Weddings Novella

Rock Springs Box Set 1-5 + Bonus Content

The Cowboy and His Mistletoe Kiss – Lilly and Mike

The Cowboy and His Valentine – Maggie and Nick

The Cowboy and His Vegas Wedding – Royce and Anna

The Cowboy and His Angel – Abby and Greg

The Cowboy and His Christmas Rockstar – Savannah and Ford

The Cowboy and His Billionaire – Brice and Kayla

Mountain Men of Whiskey River
Take Me To The River
Take Me To The Cabin
Standalone Books
Stay With Me Now
Texting Titan
Accidental Sugar Daddy
She's Still The One

Connect with Kaci Rose

Website
Facebook
Kaci Rose Reader's Facebook Group
TikTok
Instagram
Twitter
Goodreads
Book Bub
Join Kaci Rose's VIP List (Newsletter)

Please Leave a Review!

I love to hear from my readers! Please head over to your favorite store and **leave a review** of what you thought of this book!

Made in the USA
Columbia, SC
23 September 2024